STONEWORDS

2004

Merry Christmas
Maggie!
XXOO
Mommy & Daddy

ALSO BY PAM CONRAD

I DON'T LIVE HERE!

PRAIRIE SONGS

HOLDING ME HERE

WHAT I DID FOR ROMAN

SEVEN SILLY CIRCLES

TAKING THE FERRY HOME

STAYING NINE

MY DANIEL

PRAIRIE VISIONS

———

THE TUB PEOPLE

THE TUB GRANDFATHER

THE LOST SAILOR

MOLLY AND THE STRAWBERRY DAY

STONEWORDS
A Ghost Story

Pam Conrad

HarperCollins*Publishers*

Library of Congress Cataloging-in-Publication Data
Conrad, Pam.
    Stonewords: a ghost story / Pam Conrad.
        p.   cm.
    Summary: Zoe discovers that her house is occupied by the ghost of
an eleven-year-old girl, who carries her back to the day of her
death in 1870 to try to alter that tragic event.
    ISBN 0-06-021315-9.—ISBN 0-06-021316-7 (lib. bdg.)
    [1. Ghosts—Fiction.   2. Time travel—Fiction.]   I. Title.
PZ7.C76476Sw   1990   89-36382
[Fic]—dc20   CIP
                                                      AC

For my mother
and for the mother I am

Ghost Time

Never.
Not ever, at no time, on no occasion, not at all.
Nevermore, never in the world, not in a donkey's years.
Never in all one's born days,
not in my lifetime.

Time.
Lastingness, cosmic time, space-time,
timebinding.
Corridors of time, hourglass of time,
ravages of time, sweep of time.
Time's cavern.
Awhile past.

The Past.
Foretime, former times, past times, times past.
Days gone by, bygone times, yesterday.
Olden times, old days, days of old, way back.
Gone glimmering, ago, time was, old story.
Same old story . . .

STONEWORDS

1

It seems I had always woken up in the morning with leaves and bits of grass in my toes and under my sheets as if I'd been a ghost wandering the countryside at night. But maybe not. Maybe it wasn't until that summer my mother visited us when she was forever weaving honeysuckle wreaths, and I followed her out into the backwoods that night after dinner.

Now I could tell you that my mother was an exotic, mysterious woman. But fact is, she was just peculiar, maybe even a little crazy. Everyone around me knew it, and no one tried to hide it from me. I wasn't even very sensitive to it as you might suspect. Except maybe after one of her visits—which used to happen only once or twice a year—I'd get the jitters when I'd catch a glimpse of myself in the mirror, or in a window reflection and I'd see how much I looked like her. It was like pine sap—I couldn't get it off, except with time. After a couple of weeks I started to remind myself of just me again, and I'd stop thinking of her.

She had some mighty strange ways. Like she had this one cemetery on the island she loved. She didn't know anyone buried there—they'd all been dead for over a hundred years—but my mother would walk through the grass, trailing her silk scarf, with her large straw hat shading her empty eyes, and she'd pause at each stone and read the words out loud.

There was one particular double stone that always made her cry. Her voice could be as soft as the sound of a train in your sleep. "Caleb Havens, son of Augustus and Esther Havens, May 28, 1798, 1 month," and on the same stone, "Sally B. Havens, daughter of Augustus and Esther Havens, November 14, 1801, 1 year, 5 months, 10 days."

She would stand there with these soundless tears streaming down her cheeks. This mother. This mother who would come to visit us once or twice a year and take me to visit a cemetery. I grew not to expect much from her. Like birds get used to an empty bird feeder and gather to pick at the dust and chatter to each other, I was no longer surprised that there was nothing there.

I used to wander from stone to stone, idly reading

the stonewords, while I waited for her to finish, Only one stone there had any meaning for me. It had my own name. Or I should say I had its name. Grandma said my mother had fallen in love with that name on the gravestone years ago, when she was just a little girl, and that she'd always said she'd name a daughter that someday.

My name is Zoe. The stoneword on the tombstone. Zoe. Most of the face of the stone was crumbled and gone, leaving just a rutted surface where other words had been, but they were no longer readable. I used to stand before that stone to see if I felt anything. Like my mother did. But I could do it only for an instant. I didn't want to be like my mother at all. And sometimes I was scared that the only reason I wasn't like her was that I was always holding back my true self. I was a jack-in-the-box, holding the lid shut from inside with both hands. So I'd stand there by this gravestone wondering who my true self was.

I was never moved to cry, but before we'd leave, I'd always find a pebble to place on Zoe's stone, and sometimes I'd say, "It's okay, Zoe, whoever you are, it's really okay." And I'd have the queerest feeling that that would be exactly what she'd have said to me, too, if she could. And then I'd follow my mother back to her car at the edge of the road.

I can't explain why I never connected any of

this stuff with the ghost. You'll have to trust me. I just never did. For the longest time. The only possible explanation for this could be that I always tried to forget everything about my mother's visits — names, tombstones, odd mutterings. I would take a wet sponge to those visits on the blackboard of my mind. And make them vanish.

And I never had much feeling when I'd think of my mother between visits. Never loved her much. Actually I can't remember loving her at all then. Not like I loved Grandma and PopPop. Probably the strongest feeling I'd ever had for her was anger. For not being a true mother. And for not remembering what she had once told me about the rosebushes.

The ghost was in my life right from the beginning, when I first came to live on this island with Grandma and PopPop. I don't remember much about my life before I came. But from the time I entered my grandparents' safe country home everything became as clear as maple trees through a giant soap bubble. My mother brought me to their house late one hot, sweltering afternoon when I was four. I can't remember her saying good-bye, but I do recall the dark rings under her arms on her soft blouse and that her hands were like ice. I remember how she pulled Grandma's pug dog up on her lap and let it kiss her and lick her face. But after dinner, like the dirty glasses and empty mugs, she was gone.

Later, as it grew dark, Grandma, whose hands were warm, took me up the main staircase to a little bedroom at the rear of the house. She held my hand in hers, and in her other hand she carried a shopping bag with my clothes. Once we were in the room she poured the bag out onto the bed. She made soft murmuring sounds as she shuffled through the clothes, and then more gently than I had ever known, she took my clothes off me, and left me alone. I didn't move. Willing her to come back to me, not to disappear.

And she did come back with a pair of scissors and a pale white T-shirt that smelled like soap and was softer than anything of mine. Quietly she pulled it over my head, knelt at my feet, and trimmed the shirt away from the floor.

Then she led me to a bathroom that didn't echo like all the other bathrooms I'd known. All of them had been so empty, so sharp-sounding, and I'd always been drawn to them, drawn to sit on their floors for hours, calling "Ooo, hoo! Ooo, hoo!" feeling the familiar emptiness until someone told me to leave because they had to wash their dishes in the sink, or take a bath.

Here I tilted my head back and called "Ooo, hoo! Oooo, hooo!" and nothing happened. Grandma smiled at me and sang it too. "Ooo, hoo! Oooo, hooo!" Neither of us could make that empty echoing sound, and I was relieved. We laughed together and my toes sank into the thick bath mat on the floor. Grandma washed me while warm water made a quiet pond in the sink, and the white curtains hung motionless against the hot black night.

Holding my hand, she led me back to the small bedroom and helped me up onto the high bed. She told me to go to sleep now, she kissed me — put her lips to my forehead and made a little noise — and then she left me.

But the open window near my bed looked out over the backyard and soon I could hear her quiet summer voice talking to PopPop in the darkness.

I was in the house alone. It was dark.

The hall glowed a little from the light in the bathroom, but there was a quiet dripping noise that made me not want to be alone. Kneeling up on the bed, I pressed my nose to the black screen. "Grandma?" I called, not even certain that she was really out there. I heard the pug call a muffled "mfff."

"Who's calling me?" she said back.

"It's me, Zoe. I want to come out."

A moment of silence. "All right, honey. Come on out."

"I'm scared."

There was darkness and quiet and the sound of

a train in the air. Down below in the shadows, I saw Grandma's dress glowing and moving silently towards the house and the shadow of the dog prancing along behind her. I pulled my arms into the T-shirt and around my ribs and faced the door. I waited, and then I heard her footsteps on the stairs. "Come along," she called, and I slid off the bed and ran to meet her. She lifted me in her arms. I had thought I was too big to be lifted, but Grandma didn't know. She felt warm and soft and smelled like honeysuckle.

She sat me on one of her wide hips and I felt each step jolt her beneath my legs. Her hand slid down the banister like water. The screen door opened into the backyard and we entered the blackness. I could hear the giant moths throwing themselves at the windows of the house. PopPop coughed and all I could see was the orange glow of his cigarette. "So, the sandman hasn't come yet," he said.

Grandma placed me in a lawn chair between them and sat down. I could see a little now. I could see their faces, and the driveway like a dark river. I could hear the dog sigh and collapse beneath my chair, and above me I saw the powdered stars. It was warm but I tucked my feet under the edges of the T-shirt and kept my arms inside the sleeves like a turtle. I didn't like night air. There were bugs.

PopPop's face was turned up to the sky. "We're looking for shooting stars, Zoe. This is the night for them."

"There!" I shouted, pointing to the mountain of a garage in the darkness. A blink of light arched across its gaping door.

"That's a lightning bug, Zoe. Haven't you ever seen one?"

I thought a minute of the house I had been in last with my mother. Of the dark staircase in the back alley that you had to get to by passing garbage cans that swarmed with bugs. I couldn't remember ever seeing a bug make lightning. Suddenly PopPop made a big swiping movement and a clap.

"There," he said. "Got one." He rubbed the palm of his hand along the front of his shirt.

"Joe, that's terrible," Grandma said, but when he removed his hand there was a beautiful streak of the palest green glowing on his shirt. I leaned close to see, and my feet slid out of the T-shirt. And one arm. I ran a finger down the streak. My fingertip glowed too.

Grandma stood and said she would get a jar for me. I didn't know why, but PopPop caught another lightning bug, and this one he held cupped in his hands. I wanted to see, but he was still and we waited for Grandma. When she came back she un-screwed the lid and PopPop put the bug inside

8

and gave me the jar. It lit up, like a city window far off in the distance, and then it went out.

"See how many you can get, Zoe. There are hundreds out tonight." Grandma rested back in her chair and sighed. They both looked up at the sky, waiting and forgetting me.

I slid my feet down into the grass. The dark grass where there were bugs and worms and slugs, but it didn't matter. It was cool and black and a little bit wet. I walked cautiously away from my grandparents, and into my new life. My feet were bare, and a cooling breeze stole beneath my T-shirt. In my hands I held a glass jar, careful, careful, and I swear to you, even though I was only four I can feel these things as clearly as if that jar had been an offering of frankincense.

I remember the night perfectly, maybe even a little bit clearer than it actually was, and don't doubt me when I tell you that as I stood gazing into the black woods behind the garage I felt a tugging, like someone right next to me was about to laugh, but there was no one. Small hands slid over mine, over the jar, coaxing me back to the woods. Just as I had felt safe taking my grandmother's hand and following her up the stairs, so I felt safe letting my feet take me where the tugging jar led. But as I drew near the woods, where it was so dark I couldn't see my own hands, Grandma called out—

"Don't go near the woods, Zoe. There are snakes. Stay close to the house now."

I pulled the jar from those tiny tugging hands and ran back to my grandparents in their lawn chairs, and stood behind them. "Let me hold the jar, Zoe, and you bring the bugs to me." Grandma held out her hands and I gave over the jar willingly. Keeping my grandmother between the snake woods and me, I caught lightning bugs that night until my eyes were heavy and everything in the world grew slow. Some of the bugs made it into the jar and some squashed between my fingers. Then Grandma pulled me up onto her lap and I fell asleep. That was the first night that I went to bed with grass and leaves between my toes. And I can tell you honestly that while those demanding hands were never strangers to me after that night, I never went near those woods again. For a long while anyway. Not until my mother came that summer, and told me about the roses.

My grandparents' backyard was very different in the daylight than it had been beneath the stars. The bright sun revealed wide flower beds growing like cushions all around. Bumblebees obese with honey hung sleepily in the air. I walked around them.

"Oscar," PopPop said impatiently. He held the back door for the pug, who wasn't sure that he wanted to leave the kitchen. Oscar was more like a cat or a pig than any dog I'd ever seen. His face had no dog snout, but a squashed, wrinkled nose that curved in on itself, and the lines and wrinkles of his tan forehead and cheeks were edged with fine black hairs. His eyes bulged and looked outwards. "Like Emily Dickinson," Grandma liked to say.

"Come on, Oscar," I called out, feeling Oscar

could be mine now. But he wasn't. He posed on the doorstep, on three legs, his front paw raised in hesitation, alert and worried. But PopPop tucked a boot beneath the dog's tail and coaxed him out.

"The lightning bugs are sleeping," I told PopPop as he came towards me. The jar was in the grass at my feet. "They've turned their lights off."

PopPop paused beside me and looked down at the jar. "Might be a good idea to turn them free, so they can eat and get caught again tonight."

"Might be," I admitted, but I didn't touch the jar.

PopPop stood in the morning sunlight and yawned. The house framed him, the roof visible through the thin hairs on the top of his head, and had he reached out his arms from his sides, his fingers would have been even with the porch on one side, and on the other—

"What's that, PopPop?"

He turned and looked. Then smiled at me. "Why, that's a little playhouse I built for your mother a long time ago."

It was like an extra room on the house except it was too small, with a little door and little windows with faded window boxes. We walked towards it.

"I could fix it up," he said.

"Mommy's too big," I told him.

"Yes," he answered, "but you're not."

The little door opened when he punched it firmly along the edge three times. It swung open into darkness and dry leaves. He ducked and I followed him in. He had to stay crouched down and I stood full measure, and everything fit me. The windows ended at my belt. When I sat at the table, my legs didn't dangle and my arms lay perfectly across the top. There was an empty doll cradle in the corner, even a small sink, and through a little archway I could see a child-sized bed and a matching lamp.

"This is mine," said a little voice, like a voice coming down a tube.

I looked at PopPop but when he spoke his voice was right there. "Shall we fix this up for you, Zoe? Would you like that?"

"Oh, yes. And I can live here!"

"It's mine," repeated the voice.

"Well, you can certainly play out here to your heart's content, but you'll live with Grandma and me in the big house. You can play here all the time."

"Can I sleep out here?"

"Mine."

"Well, I don't know. Your mother used to take naps out here. You can do that."

"And will it be mine?" Something kicked my shin lightly and I looked under the table. A little brown shoe with buttons tapped impatiently. Over the table, a little girl, older than I was, frowned.

"Of course it will be yours. If you'll help me fix it up. Will you do that?"

I nodded. The girl wore a lavender cotton dress with tiny pink buttons, and her hair was neatly parted in the center and bound in two thick braids. Below each ear was an enormous, fussy bow. I had never seen a little girl so pretty before. Or so translucent. She was like a block of ice that I could see, and see through at the same time. She nodded, too.

"Both of us," I told her.

"Both of us," PopPop answered. "You can sweep and dust, and I'll hammer and wash." He left me there and ducked out the door. No sooner was he gone than a little broom spun from the corner where it was standing and danced across the room throwing leaves and pollynoses all around until—for the first time since I had arrived—I laughed out loud.

I'll bet PopPop heard me that morning, laughing like that. And I'll bet he thought I was feeling pretty happy with the little house and that I'd be just fine without my mother.

Grandma and PopPop worked for days on the little house, as if they'd forgotten it was there and, suddenly discovering it, thought it could bring something back. I remember the hammering, and painting, the prying and grunting, and I would sit in the grass outside with the pretty girl. I never tried to hide her in those days from my grandparents. It never occurred to me. After all, she'd sit right beside me. In the open.

"Zoe Louise wants the inside pink," I told my grandmother.

"You like pink?" my grandmother asked.

"No. I like blue, but Zoe Louise likes pink and I promised her she could have pink. Her birthday's coming, you know."

"Zoe Louise," my grandmother said thoughtfully.

"She likes pink. That's what she said."

"And where is this Zoe Louise?"

"She went home. Her papa's bringing her a pony."

Grandma nodded. "I see. Well, pink it will be. If that's what you want."

"Zoe Louise wants pink."

So PopPop painted the inside pink, and on the walls he made little white shelves for the small china dishes. And I played in the playhouse all my summers with Zoe Louise to keep me company. I would wash the dishes in the little sink that ran real water, water that Grandma carried from the kitchen in a milk bottle. And Zoe Louise would dry them and put them back on the shelf all crooked.

I always had to fix them. I'd look out the window over the sink with its gray-and-white curtains that had red roosters on them and tell Zoe Louise to see the leaves turning red and orange in the cold, and wasn't it a good day to be indoors. On the pretend stove with its painted flames I would keep a real teapot with juice in it for us, and on the table Grandma would come and place a bowl of small red apples, or sometimes a bowl of cherries.

"I have to go home now," Zoe Louise said one afternoon. "Momma thinks I'm off with Oliver."

"Oliver?"

"My brother."

"I'd like a brother someday."

She looked at me in horror. "Whatever for? He's terrible. He's always dirty. His nose runs. He keeps frogs and bird skulls in his pockets and he smells bad."

"Where do you go?" I asked, popping a cherry into my mouth. "Where do you live with your brother?"

"Up the stairs."

"What stairs?"

"In the house."

I stopped chewing. "But that's my room up there."

She stood and walked to the door. "Not *those* stairs. The others."

She passed through the closed door to the outside

and as she did, a couple of leaves swirled through her and settled on the floor. I opened the solid door and felt the cold autumn air blow through every tiny hole of my knitted sweater. She strode ahead, her arms bare, her braids bouncing down her back, and her brown button shoes kicking up leaves.

"Momma's calling! Maybe Papa's back," she said over her shoulder, and she started to run. I tried to keep up. She flew in the back door of the house and into the kitchen. I was a few steps behind her, but too late. When I stepped into the kitchen she was gone. Not a sound. Not a footstep, not a leaf, nothing. Just Grandma sitting at the table slicing string beans into her heavy pot, with Oscar at her feet like a cement garden toad.

"You see Zoe Louise, Grandma?"

She smiled at me. "I thought she was out in the playhouse with you, dear." The string beans clunked into the pot.

"Her mother was calling her. She lives up the stairs." I climbed onto the big chair next to her.

"I see. The back stairs?"

I stared at her.

"Where I keep the vacuum cleaner?" She pointed to a door next to the refrigerator—a door I looked at every day, because it had a little bird right in

17

the middle, a bird that turned red if it was going to rain, blue if it was going to be sunny. But I'd never seen anyone open the door.

I slid off my seat and approached it, touched the doorknob, then clasped it in two hands and pulled. The door opened. A chill ran over my feet. Like the legs of a scarecrow, two metal vacuum-cleaner tubes toppled out into the room at my feet. I stepped over them and in the darkness saw the stone steps leading up into blackness.

"What's up there, Grandma?"

"The hall upstairs. By the linen closet." She was rinsing the beans in the sink but she heard me step over the vacuum and start up the stairs. "No, no, Zoe. Don't go up that way. It's all dusty and spidery. And the stones are loose. We don't use that staircase anymore."

"Why?"

"We don't use it, that's all. The other staircase is fine. Use that if you have to go upstairs."

I thought I heard voices coming from the top of the stairs. A woman's voice, maybe. And a brother's. I tore from the kitchen, through the dining room, and up the stairs in the living room. I opened one door and shelves of towels and sheets and blankets towered above me. It smelled like soap. I closed it and opened the next door and again felt the cold chill run over my feet. The stairway was faintly lit by the open door at the bottom, and I could see the vacuum cleaner spread out on the floor down there.

Grandma's head peeked up at me. "I see you."

"Where's Zoe Louise, Grandma? She's gone." I started to cry.

Grandma's face melted, gazing up at me. "Oh, come now. Come down by Grandma, and bring a book. Zoe Louise will come back. You know that. She always does."

Zoe Louise always comes back, I said to myself, as I started down the main staircase with a thin book under my arm. That was right. Zoe Louise always came back.

While I could always count on Zoe Louise to come back sooner or later, I could never be sure when or where I'd find her. If I felt like playing house and the air was brisk and my dolls were soft, and my socks smelled comfortably familiar when I climbed onto the little bed, then Zoe Louise would just about always be there. She'd bring her own dolls, but she'd want to be the mother to my dolls. Her dolls were ugly, some without faces, and the ones that did have faces looked like old people and not at all like babies, and I'd have to be their mother. My dolls had soft plastic faces that smelled like love, and even their little fingers tasted good.

I had booties that fit their feet, and bottles that fit the tiny holes in their lips.

"I don't want to be mother to your ugly old dolls," I told her one day. "I want my own."

"That's not polite," she pouted. "I'm the guest, and you're not being polite to me."

"You're always the guest. I'm always polite. When do I get to be the guest?"

"I'm the guest now," she insisted. "And I want this baby. I think you should give me this one for my birthday." She scooped my baby doll up out of the cradle by its leg, and I had had enough of her being my guest. I dove for the doll. I slid right through Zoe Louise's body as she held the doll in the air over my head.

"You let me play with it," she demanded. "Or I'm going home."

I thought a minute. "Go home," I said. I held open the door to the little house and she stormed out. With my baby doll. "Leave my doll," I said, but she was running across the lawn back to the house. "Zoe Louise!" I shouted. I ran after her, my eyes glued to my baby doll that she was waving around by its foot. She bounded up the wooden back steps and this time I was right at her heels. I was right behind her. In time to see her pass through the back door—and with a loud punching jolt, she was stopped by my baby doll who was held against the door by only her slightly visible hand. I grabbed my doll and pulled. On the other side of the door, she pulled.

"It's mine!" I shouted.

"Mine!" I could hear her.

"No, mine! Mine!"

"Zoe, dear." It was Grandma, just as the leg tore off the baby doll's body and Zoe Louise's invisible hand disappeared through the door. Grandma opened the door and she stood there alone. My doll was torn in two. "Oh, Zoe. What have you done? Why aren't you more careful with your things?"

3

Sometimes we fought. And sometimes we got along like best friends, like something out of a book where everything is perfect and people are always kind and smiling. It could really be like that for us, and I guess that's why I grew to love her as much as I did. But things were always changing. Except for Zoe Louise herself, who didn't seem to be growing older, as I was.

When Zoe Louise first came into my life I was four, and she was much older than that. I could tell, because she was a head taller, and already knew the ways of being bossy. But as I grew older, she seemed to stay the same. And when I was ten our eyes were level with each other's, and once that happened she would do this strange thing where we would stand face-to-face for long periods of time. She liked to do that, and I did it because she wanted to, and because I liked her to stay with me.

She'd stop right in the middle of something—playing dolls, brushing Oscar, running across the lawn—clasp my shoulders hard, and stare into my eyes. We'd stand face-to-face and she'd stare into my eyes like that as though there was tiny print in the backs of my pupils that she was trying to read. I always let her. Sometimes we stood in the middle of the little house like that. Sometimes we sat knee-to-knee on the lawn this way. I was always patient.

Except once.

We were out in the snow, building a snowman by the garage one morning. Icicles hung like giant ballerina legs from the edge of the roof, and the hard sun in a gray sky kept them all dripping and sparkling. I was nearly eleven, familiar by now with every corner and drawer and leaf pile in my grandparents' house and yard. Even Oscar was at last mine. I was the only one who could stand his snoring at night, and I loved to feel his warm sleeping body up against me.

Oscar was in the house this day, sitting on the back of a chair by the window, gazing out at me. If I waved and called his name, his head would cock to one side and he would paw at the window.

Grandma called out to me to stop teasing him. I said send him out, but Oscar wouldn't walk in snow. And on snowy days, before the paths were worn, Oscar would leave what Grandma called "messages" for her around the house. A little pile under the dining-room table. A little puddle on the bathroom floor.

"What a stupid dog," Zoe Louise said. She was patting the shoulder of the snowman with bare hands.

"He's not stupid. He's smart. Who'd want to come out naked in the snow? No clothes. No boots. I bet if we got him a dog coat he'd come out."

"That's the most ridiculous thing I ever heard."

I looked at Zoe Louise thoughtfully. I patted the head into the snowman's shoulders. To her it probably was ridiculous. After all I was bundled in sweaters and scarves and a coat and mittens, and she wore the same light cotton dress she'd always worn even in the summer, with brown button shoes and bare arms.

"Aren't you cold?" I asked, not for the first time.

She looked at me shrewdly. "It's no big deal to be naked in the snow." She clapped her hands together as if to brush off the snow and suddenly stood apart from me and the snowman. In one movement she pulled her dress up over her head and draped it over the snowman, slipped out of her pale-gray underwear, and stood there bare-naked

24

in the white snow in just her blue cotton socks and her thin button shoes. Her body was just like mine, skinny legs, a round belly, and a chest as flat as an unread book.

I glanced back at the house, forgetting for a moment that Grandma and PopPop had never really seen Zoe Louise, had always gotten that patient sound to their voices when I talked about her. So much so that I had stopped talking about her a long time ago. And they thought I had outgrown her. Even when I would talk directly to Zoe Louise I had learned to stop moving my mouth, in case they were watching. I knew Zoe Louise could understand me even if I said the words only in my head.

But now I spoke out loud. "Put your clothes on. Before someone sees you!"

"No one can see me. Only you."

"Well, put them on." I glanced back at the house and Oscar was pressing his face to the window, and I couldn't hear him but I could tell he was barking and getting frantic. "Oscar sees you."

"So? What's he going to do? Call the governor?" She started skipping around the snowman, passing through the icicles, brushing her fingers over the top of my head. "Come on, Zoe. Dance naked with me in the snow."

I stood up and backed away from her and the snowman. Zoe Louise had forced me to do many things over the years—share dolls, get her more cherries, let her braid my hair—but she wouldn't get me to do this.

She came after me, light and agile in the snow, as I clambered backwards in Grandma's boots that were too big. Snow seeped down my ankles, my fingers were stiff with cold. She was on me in no time, her hands squeezing my shoulders, her eyes level with mine, that sudden peering for messages in the darkest corners of my brain, only this time I wouldn't let her do it.

"No!" I shouted at her, turning my head and looking away. "No!"

"Look at me," she demanded.

But this time, I wouldn't. I squeezed my eyes shut.

"Look at me! Look at me!" she yelled. "Let me see!"

But I pulled away, yanked my shoulders from her grip, and ran back to the house with a sob crowding my throat.

I stayed in my room the rest of the afternoon, cutting out paper dolls, dressing them, and standing them on the drafty windowsills and along the edge of my bedspread on the floor. I could feel her fury in the air of the house, hear her silent rage in the quiet hiss of the radiators.

"Zoe!" PopPop called. "Chow time!"

I had smelled the pot roast first, the warm, rich, brown smell woven with vegetables and herbs that seeped into my room like the sound of a distant cello, and then the smell of hot biscuits had come like a marching band.

"Coming!" I called. When I opened the door to my room, the paper dolls toppled over and their dresses and suits came undone. Glancing nervously at the back-stairway door out of the corner of my eye, I slammed my door behind me and slipped past the stairway door tucking my hands across my behind as if I expected to be hit. I ran down the stairs.

But Zoe Louise wasn't hiding behind the back-stairway door, and she wasn't out in the backyard, naked and waiting. I knew this because I looked as I passed the window. Only the unfinished snow-man stood pale and still in the early darkness. No, Zoe Louise was standing in the middle of the dining-room table, fully dressed now, except that her buttons were buttoned wrong, her one braid was caught over her ear, and both her feet seemed planted in the pot roast. Her arms were crossed over her chest and she was glaring at me.

"Where were you?" she demanded.

"In my room," I answered out loud.

Grandma glanced at me as she carried the bowl

of corn and the butter dish to the table. "Is it warm enough up there, dear?"

"You know it's hard for me to find you when you go in your room," Zoe Louise said.

"Yes, Grandma." I answered. "It's warm."

"Radiator hot?" PopPop asked, snapping out his thick linen napkin and smoothing it across his lap.

I kept my lips shut tight. *I didn't want you to find me, stupid. Stupid, naked girl who doesn't have the sense to stay warm in a blizzard.*

She stamped her foot hard in the pot roast bowl and phantom drops of gravy splattered in the air. Grandma and PopPop seemed not to notice.

"Zo?" PopPop was peering at me over the tops of his glasses.

"What?"

"I asked if the radiator was hot."

Zoe Louise began marching around the table, her knees high, her feet sinking into the bowls and silverware. Spoons clattered in their bowls, biscuits flattened to shadows beneath her shoes, and the chandelier began a shrill vibration as her ghostly head passed through it.

"I just wanted you to look in my eyes!" she shouted.

I pressed my palm over my mouth and stared through my fingers.

"Zoe!" It was PopPop.

"Yes! Yes! The radiator's hot."

My grandparents gave each other a look over the neat bowl of pot roast and the little pile of perfect biscuits. They couldn't see what was going on. But Oscar could.

He stood up by the table, his front feet on my chair, and growled. The hair stood up in a wide ridge down the center of his back. It ended at his tail that curled back like a party horn. "Sit," I whispered to him.

"What's wrong with Oscar?" Grandma asked, beginning to dish out the pot roast, first on PopPop's plate, then mine.

"I think he can feel the blizzard in the air," PopPop told her. He broke open a biscuit and the steam escaped into the soft light. "I think we all can. Something about the air, the atmosphere. Makes my knees hurt."

"Some corn, dear?" Grandma held a huge spoon of corn over my plate.

"Won't you please just look in my eyes. Just for a little while."

"Yes," I answered, and the spoon of corn and Zoe Louise's behind landed in my dish at exactly the same instant. "I mean, no!"

"Oh please, Zoe, just eat it. You like corn. Joe, corn?"

Zoe Louise sat on my plate facing me, her legs

crossed, her brown button shoes scattering corn on the table and on my lap and she leaned close to peer into my eyes. I put my hands over them and ducked my head. I didn't move my lips. I gritted my teeth. *Not now*, I told her.

"Good idea, Zoe," PopPop said. "Let's say grace this evening." He bowed his head and Grandma sat down heavily.

I could feel Zoe Louise's chin on my head. "When?" she asked.

"Dear Lord, bless this food, this house, these loved ones, and keep everyone safe tonight on the slippery roads."

When I'm done eating, I said silently.

"Amen," Grandma answered.

"Amen," Zoe Louise echoed, suddenly sitting up straight. "My papa's coming home soon. Are the roads slippery? He's bringing me a pony, you know."

I looked at her. I could see where tears had streaked her cheeks. They were dried and dirty.

"Zoe, pass the biscuits, please," PopPop said.

I lifted the basket and Zoe lifted it with me, her fingers gentle on mine, helping me.

Go away, I told her silently. *Go wait on the stairs.*

"The back stairs?"

No, the stairs to my room.

PopPop looked puzzled and thanked me.

"You won't forget, will you? I have to get home. Papa's coming."

I shook my head and Zoe Louise stood up on the table. As she stepped off, the hem of her dress caught on the edge of my milk glass. I reached for it, it tipped, and milk spilled in a wave over my dish and down the side of the tablecloth.

Grandma leaped up. "Goodness, Zoe! Your head is in the clouds today." She hurried into the kitchen and came out with a thick towel to sop it all up.

4

Zoe Louise was waiting on the stairs when I was done. And I had taken as long as I could, even though I could tell she was restless by the way Oscar was worrying himself from room to room. Grandma and PopPop kept looking out the window into the thick, heavy darkness until they seemed relieved to suddenly see snow swirling around once again.

When I finally took the stairs two at a time, PopPop was building a fire in the large stone fireplace, and Zoe Louise was at my heels.

"It's my birthday, you know, and Papa's bringing me a pony."

"You told me already. A hundred times. You're always saying that." I threw myself on my bed and pulled the quilt up around my shoulders.

"Sit up," she said, dropping beside me.

I didn't move.

"You promised," she said, her voice laced with fear.

I looked at her. "What's the big deal? I don't like to do that anymore."

"You like it," she said, tugging me up, turning me to face her, our knees touching. "You just forget."

She held my shoulders then, and surrendering, I let her look into my eyes. Sometimes during the winter months when the trees were bare in the backwoods, I used to watch the lighthouse out by Mulvey Point from the east window in my grandparents' attic, and in the darkness I could count to seven slowly and at each seven its light would flash through the night into my eyes. Zoe Louise's eyes were like that, only the seven went on and on, not passing by, but flashing and staying. Holding me pinned to the moment.

She looked and she looked and she looked. The room glowed with silent snow. And I watched her looking, wishing I could get up and look with her into the blackness of my own eyes. What did she see?

"What are you looking at?" I asked her, her face as close as a dentist's.

"For," she corrected me. "For."

"Well, what are you looking for?"

33

"I'm looking for the truth. To see if you know."

"If I know what?"

She was silent, her eyes still, her summery breath tickling my upper lip. After a while, she closed her eyes and leaned away from me. She seemed neither happy nor disappointed when it was over. Kind of like someone who fishes not to catch fish, but to just be quiet. It was done.

"If I know what?" I repeated.

"You don't know," she told me. "When you know, you will know, and when I look into your eyes, then I'll know, too."

"What are you talking about?" I asked angrily. I stood up and began jamming all my paper dolls back into their shoe box.

"I'm not sure," she whispered. She picked up a paper doll of a lady in a long ball gown and ran her fingers over it. "I'd better go home," she said, glancing at the closed door, but she didn't move. She just sat there. Usually, once Zoe Louise thought of going home, there was no stopping her. She'd just be gone. But this time she sat on my bed and seemed uneasy. A hard wind began pelting the window with snow and a cold draft danced around the room, despite the hissing radiator.

"So, just go."

"I'm scared."

"Of what?"

She shrugged. "Walk me to the stairs."

She had never asked me to do that before. Never. I had never once seen her disappear up the stairs. She'd always be gone when I got there. I could tell she really was frightened.

"All right."

"Bring a candle," she said, standing. "It's dark on the stairs." And then she walked through my door.

I reached beneath my pillow and grabbed the flashlight that I used at night to read by, and quickly bolted out of my room, afraid that she would disappear like always. She was not at the top of the back stairs. The door was closed tight. I placed my ear against it and heard nothing. Only the sound of Grandma and PopPop watching television in the living room.

"Down here," I heard her whisper, and I saw the wispy shadow of her disappear down the main stairs. I followed as quietly as I could, skipping steps that I knew would squeak under my weight. I slipped past the living room where my grandmother sat knitting and my grandfather was filling the air with pipe smoke. The kitchen was all wiped and put away for the night, the damp dish towel hanging neatly over the edge of the counter, and the only light was the purple light kept lit over Grandma's African violets.

"Open the door," Zoe Louise whispered.

I did as she told me, ready to catch the vacuum-cleaner tubes that spilled out at us. "Shhhhh," I scolded, nearly dropping the flashlight.

Zoe Louise stepped past me into the bottom of the stairway. She stood there with her arms wrapped around herself, staring up into the darkness as if she were suddenly cold. "Where's your light?" she whispered.

Then Grandma called from the living room. "Zoe? Is that you?"

Without thinking I leaped into the stairway after Zoe Louise and pulled the door tight behind me. We were in total blackness. And being so close I was partially through her. Her transparent heart beat inside my arm like a trembling bird. We could hear Grandma come into the room talking to Oscar. "Where's that girl?" she was saying. "Just when an old fellow needs a cookie." We listened to her open a cabinet and spill out a dog biscuit. "There you go, old boy." There were a few small noises, the water in the sink ran, a flowerpot was turned. And then her disappearing footsteps.

I flicked on the flashlight and Zoe Louise was still standing there, her arms tight around herself and her face turned towards the top of the stairs. "Momma's calling," she said.

I shone the beam of light up the steps. "Go. Go on home."

She turned to look at me. The light did funny things to her, making her face look like a soft jellyfish that I could see right through to the hair down her back. The bones in her fingers showed like little neons, glowing. She didn't move.

"Come with me," she pleaded. "It's my birthday. You can come."

I shook my head no. Never. The hair stood up on my arms. Even my eyebrows prickled like static.

"Just partway," she begged. "I'm afraid."

"You were never afraid before."

"I know. I know. Now I am afraid." She took a step, then another up the stairs. I had never seen her like this. She curled her fingers around my wrist and pulled me with her. I stepped up one step. Another step. The flashlight showed nothing unusual. Just the top of the stairs. I could open the door at the top and find the linen closet there, and my room. Couldn't I?

"Do you hear her?" she asked me.

"Grandma?" I cocked my head, wondering if Grandma'd come back and would find me in the staircase.

"No. My mother. She's looking for me."

There was a snorting under the bottom door. Oscar knew where I was. He breathed deep and noisily, inhaling the air for my scent. He knew exactly where I was, and in one minute, he'd start crying and scratching at the door. "I gotta go," I said, squirming my arm out of her grasp, and I backed down the stairs, still holding the light for her. She seemed to turn to smoke on the stairs, to smoke and to flesh, back and forth as if wavering.

"It's cold," she said, rubbing her smoky arms.

"Go on. Go ahead," I pleaded. "You'll be all right."

Then as if someone had lit a fire under her, she bolted up the remaining stairs, burst open the door at the top, and slammed it behind her. I stood there alone, stunned. I thought to go up another step. I thought to just peek through the door at the top and see what was there. I can't quite explain why I didn't then. Any more than I can explain why I had begun one day to let my grandparents believe that Zoe Louise had gone away for good and I didn't see her anymore. Even though I did. Maybe I was afraid they were starting to think I was crazy. Maybe they'd start to think I was like my mother. There on the staircase, I wondered if I *was* crazy.

Oscar started scratching on the door. I turned off the flashlight and opened the door into the lavender glow. I wasn't crazy. I was as sane as you think you are. Even Oscar knew that. When I bent down to pat him he pressed his nose into my wrist, the wrist that Zoe Louise had clasped, and Oscar sniffed intently, decoding and figuring in his dog brain what he thought might have been there. Oscar was like my weather vane. I would have almost disbelieved myself, doubted there was any of this wind at all, but then I'd see him turn into it, and I'd know that Oscar was seeing the same things I was seeing.

I didn't see Zoe Louise for a long time after that. I figured from what she told me that maybe she had had her birthday and didn't need me anymore now that she had her pony. But it wasn't so. I was soon to learn that what to me seemed like months and weeks — while the days were going from glaring white ice to tender green buds — all that time was only a moment to Zoe Louise.

I didn't see her again for a couple of years. And then it was I who went looking for *her*. It was spring, and I found her wearing the same lavender dress with the tiny pink buttons, still waiting for her father to bring her the pony. But I hadn't gone looking for her till I finally knew the truth of things, or part of the truth. The truth she'd been looking for in my eyes. And it was my own mother who told me.

5

Honeysuckle has been known to bloom in the snow. It has its own internal time schedule that has nothing to do with wind, weather, or season. It's as if honeysuckle were always daydreaming, coming out of deep thought to say something so off and disconnected that everyone around is confused and thrown off-balance. My mother was like this.

She would sit at the dining-room table with my grandparents and me, Oscar curled at her feet, and if you were to take a picture, you'd think, this is nice. Looks okay. You wouldn't be able to tell that she just drove up an hour ago and that no one had heard a word from her for six months before that. Or that she had hugged me woodenly before scooping up old Oscar and letting him lick and nibble at her face as if she were *his* mother with a treat held in her teeth. She'd clamp her lips shut and her eyes, and laugh deep in her throat.

We had a midafternoon dinner as we always did on Sundays. My mother sat with her one leg crossed over the other, her foot twitching. Any minute she could leave. She smoked a long, thin cigarette that she spun in the ashtray, whittling the glowing tip to a fine hot point.

"I got a job with a country-craft place," she was telling Grandma. PopPop had gone inside, so it was just the three of us left at the table. I sat on my hands and watched her. "Making wreaths and quilted things, and flower arrangements."

Grandma leaned against the wooden back of her chair, its carved leaves framing her gray head. She studied her daughter. "I never knew you to like that kind of thing, Jessie."

My mother shrugged. "It's good work. I make my own hours. The people don't nag me. I show up when I show up."

"Such a blessing," my grandmother answered, and I could taste her bitterness in the way she began to stack the dishes. *I show up when I show up.* I started to stack my dish and my glass when my mother looked at me and spoke directly into my eyes.

"Would you like to go back in the woods and

help me gather some honeysuckle vines for wreaths before it gets dark?"

I felt my face grow hot. I didn't know what to say to her.

"Go on, Zoe," my grandmother coaxed. "I'll take care of these tonight."

We stood and backed up from the table in unison, my mother and I. If I had stood right next to her, I would have reached her shoulder. If I'd had a mind to, my arms could've circled her waist. If she'd thought to, her chin could have rested on the top of my head. We went to get our jackets.

"Take Oscar with you, Zoe," my grandmother called, heading into the kitchen with a stack of dishes. "He hasn't been out in a while."

It was growing cold out, even though the earlier day had been warm, and it smelled like thawing ground and new air. I lifted Oscar and carried him down the back steps. His old age made steps precarious for him, and from the top he would look like a pig walking down the stairs headfirst.

"He's too old for the stairs," I explained to my mother, when she frowned at me.

"He was always too fat," she said, rubbing his neck as I held him in my arms.

"He's not too fat," I snapped. "Pugs are like that. They're supposed to be just like Oscar."

"Hmm."

She walked ahead while I set Oscar down on the brown grass. I stared at her back. Why should I go find honeysuckle with *her*? I looked back at the house to see Grandma and PopPop standing at the dining-room window. PopPop turned away, and Grandma motioned me to go on.

My mother was heading back to the garage, past the garage to the snake woods. Her arms swung at her sides and she tipped her head back to look up into the trees. I dug my fists into my jacket pockets and went after her. Without breaking stride she continued on into the woods, her step as sure through the brambles as it had been over the lawn. I had never set foot here before. I had accepted the limit as though this property belonged to someone else and there had been a fence. I looked back but couldn't see anyone in the house anymore. Oscar was watering the abandoned snow shovel. We went deeper and deeper into the woods until she stopped to poke around. A huge tree stump that came to her waist was covered with bare honcysuckle vines. She began to unwind them from the stump and wind them about her arm, from her fist to her elbow, making a big circle.

Then she was still and her face went puzzled. She looked at me. "What was this for again?"

"What?"

"These vines. What did I need them for?"

43

I kept my face blank. "Wreaths, you said."

"Oh, yes. Yes."

I looked away from her and back towards the house. I couldn't see it. Or the neighboring houses. There was a thickness in the woods that blocked out sound and surroundings and even light. I walked deeper, deeper, until my jeans caught on something and my legs were suddenly entangled in thorns.

"Shoot," I said, bending to pull the thorns from my jeans, but the more I struggled, the more they seemed to cling to me, and my fingers were pricked over and over. I sucked on my finger that bled a dark-red drop.

"What did you do, find the rosebushes?" My mother was looking at me.

"These can't be rosebushes out here," I answered. "But it's something. It's full of—ouch—thorns and they're all over me."

She came and stood near, but didn't help me pull the long prickly vines off. She watched as I struggled. "The memory roses," she said as if that explained it all.

"What are you talking about now?" I snapped, backing away and pulling thorns one at a time from my jeans.

"These are the memory roses that were planted when that little girl died."

She swept her hand the width of the place and

for the first time I could see a straight stand of shrubs, obviously an intentional planting, not wild at all. "What little girl?" I asked.

She reached forward and pinched a rose vine between her fingers, as if to test it for a wreath. But she flinched and sucked her finger. "The people who built this house, years ago, over a hundred years maybe, they had a little girl who died."

She turned then and began walking deeper into the woods, looking for her honeysuckle. The hair stood up on the back of my neck.

"How'd she die?" I called after her, stumbling, suddenly not wanting her to leave me now.

I saw her shrug.

"Was she sick?"

"I don't know. No. I think there was an accident. I don't remember."

"Why rosebushes?"

"Oh, they said her mother was so heartbroken when she died that she planted a bank of roses along the back here, pink roses, the little girl's favorite color, so that in the spring they would always bloom on her birthday. That's the story I heard." She shrugged again. "I don't know."

"So these rosebushes are over a hundred years old?"

"I guess so. If the story's true."

We came to a break in the trees where the sun

45

streamed from the west, warm and almost springlike. It was bright and harsh, the light that I saw my mother in. The skin around her eyes looked loose as she concentrated on her thin vines. I stared at her. I wanted to pin her down and watch her face when I asked the next question.

"What was her name, Mommy?"

My mother looked up at me, startled as I was, I think, that I had called her that, called her anything at all. Like it would have been less shocking if I had called her Jessie.

The sunset wind swept through the trees drawing strings of her beige hair across her lips. "Zoe. Zoe something. That was the name I had seen on the old tombstone, but it was mostly worn off."

I was watching Oscar coming towards us, picking his way through the brambles, prancing along in his old, fat gait, leaving his signature here and there. "I gotta get back," I said. "Oscar shouldn't be coming back here. It's dangerous. There are snakes."

"There are no snakes back here. Zoe! Come back! Where are you going? Zoe!"

I heard my mother's voice following me as I ran out of the woods, calling that name—Zoe, Zoe, and I knew the rest—Zoe Louise. I scooped Oscar up in my arms and carried him back to the house, pretending I was a shepherd and he was my fat lamb that I had saved from the wilds. I buried my face in his furry neck and smelled him, taking comfort from his sweet popcorn smell. "You stay away from there, Oscar, you hear?" I told him. "You stay away from there."

My mother left soon after dark, and my grandparents went to bed early. The house creaked in the darkness and in the cold. I lay flat on my back staring at the ceiling, listening to the branch outside my window rub against the gutter, listening to Oscar snoring. So that's where Zoe Louise had gone. My Zoe Louise was dead. Tears ran from the corners of my eyes down into my ears. I had never wanted her to die. Not at all. I had wanted her to stop staring into my eyes, and stop teasing and stop disappearing, but not die. Not my beautiful Zoe Louise, my first friend.

I couldn't stand it anymore. Quietly I reached under my pillow until I felt the flashlight and slowly drew the covers back from my legs. Oscar didn't even move. He went on snoring, his eyes rolled back somewhere deep in his furrowed brow.

I tiptoed to the door, opened it without a sound, and closed it behind me. A tiny night-light flickered at the top of the main stairs, and by its dim spark I found my way down the steps to the living room, and then by the lavender light of Grandma's plant light I walked silently into the kitchen. My feet were bare and the linoleum stung like ice, but I didn't want to go back. A clean terror ran through my blood and wouldn't let me stop. At the door to the back staircase I hesitated. Wiped my sweaty palm along the length of my flannel nightgown and then, ready to catch the vacuum tubes, I opened the door. The vacuum wasn't there. The floor was dusty under my feet as I slipped in. I closed the door behind me and lit the flashlight with trembling hands.

I started up the steps. They felt gritty beneath my feet, and I maneuvered over loose pieces of stone that threatened to slip away. Higher and higher, closer and closer to the top door. A light shone underneath, as though it were daytime, and the sun was shining. I could hear sounds, talking, laughter. It was Zoe Louise, and I smiled. She was all right.

I reached for the doorknob and my hand and arm disappeared through the door up to my elbow, and I nearly tumbled through, like lifting a pitcher you think is heavy only to find it empty. I threw myself back against the wall, gasping. I touched myself, my arms, my chest. I was solid. I was sure of it, and yet as I reached out once again to the doorknob, I passed through it as if my body were no more than smoke.

I braced myself, stood the flashlight at my feet, took a deep breath, and with both hands leading, pressed through the door, my hands and my wrists all disappearing from me, my forearms, my elbows gone, and then I pressed my face to the door. Nothing resisted. Nothing stopped me. My face pushed through the door like the most natural thing in the world until I was halfway through up to my waist. I froze in terror.

The upstairs hall was bright. Sun streamed through the windows, there was light everywhere, pale curtains, flowers, and instead of linoleum on the floor as Grandma and PopPop had in the hall, there was polished wood the color of browning butter. The smell was wonderful, like wax and spring and chocolate melting somewhere.

Suddenly Zoe Louise burst into the hall before me. Zoe Louise and a woman in a full-skirted long dress that rustled when she walked.

"Oh!" Zoe Louise said when she saw me. The woman kept walking. She hadn't noticed me there protruding from the door like a souvenir elk head.

"Oh, you've come!" Zoe Louise said excitedly. I noticed her dress was clean and buttoned straight and her hair was neat, and she was as clean and shining as if she had just been fussed over.

"Come along, Zoe Louise, love. Let's see how the cake is coming."

"But Zoe's here, Momma! Zoe's coming! She's coming to my birthday party!"

The woman stood at the top of the main staircase

and looked back at her daughter. A look of bewilderment passed over her face, but she still didn't seem to notice me there. And then someone called from downstairs.

"Mrs. LaBarge! Oh, Mrs. LaBarge! Could you come here a minute, please?"

"Coming, Alethea," the woman said, and I could see she was beautiful, and happy. She turned back to Zoe Louise and smiled, a flash of delight cutting across her face. "Stop your nonsense, Zoe Louise," she whispered, "and come help Alethea decorate your cake."

"But, Momma—" Zoe Louise reached out to me.

Mrs. LaBarge pursed her lips, lowered her eyes, and without another word lifted her skirts before her and disappeared down the main stairs.

Zoe Louise's fingers wound loosely around my wrist. "Come," she pleaded. "Come!"

But I pulled back. "Stop it. She doesn't know I'm here, can't you see that? Just like Grandma and you." The idea of someone not seeing me frightened me. Zoe Louise's mother hadn't seen me there. If I had spoken she wouldn't have heard me. I was invisible. It was daytime, yet I knew it was night. None of this made sense and I felt like I couldn't breathe. I kept pulling back, folding into the door.

"Zoe, come back!" I heard her call from the other side. I hesitated the slightest instant. I wanted to be with her. But then I turned and tore down the stairs, kicking the flashlight before me. The door at the top opened and threw light streaming down the staircase. Zoe Louise leaned into the stairwell and called after me, over and over. I could hear her as I ran through the kitchen.

"Zoe! Zoe!" Her voice followed me as I tore up the main stairs, but when I flung open my door and took a flying leap across the room and into my bed, it stopped. Oscar snorted and rolled over. I was staring at my ceiling once again. Only this time my heart was pounding in my ears.

I touched things. My headboard, the wall, the mattress, my pillow. I made sure I was real, that I didn't pass through things, that I was not a ghost. Was not a ghost. I wasn't a ghost anymore.

6

I t   w a s   j u s t   a week or so later.
PopPop had been out working in the garden, raking
out flower beds for Grandma, sweeping out the
garage, and carrying trash to the back of the pickup.
Everywhere there was pale green pushing up through
the hard soil. The lawn seemed tender with the
faintest breath of new strands hardly visible, and
the dogwood buds were tiny baby fists swollen to
bursting.

When PopPop came in the back door he stomped
his feet and tiny clods of dirt loosened from his
boots. "I was thinking of opening up the playhouse,
Zoe," he said. "Think you might be too big for it
this year?"

"Never, Pop. How could I be too big?" I was
at the sink, washing the lunch dishes for Grandma

when he came and stood by me. He smelled fresh like wind in the trees.

"Well, I can't stand up in that house," he said, "and look at the size you've taken on this winter." He stooped over till his shoulder was even with mine.

"I'll get in even if I have to crawl in on my hands and knees," I said, and I meant it. I was sure that I would always go there with a book and a can of soda, to lie on the little bed and read or dream, or maybe wait for Zoe Louise. If she should ever come again.

"Okay," he said. "Just checking before I go to any great pains, and then discover you're too big for it. You promise you're still going to go in there this summer?"

"I promise, PopPop. Cross my heart and hope to die."

"Well, come on out when you're done and give me a hand." PopPop ducked into the stone staircase and came out with the vacuum cleaner and the tubes and hoses. "Bring some window cleaner with you, and wood polish—"

"PopPop!" I moaned. Grandma had just given me a string of spring-cleaning chores to do in the house. But PopPop ignored me and left, banging the vacuum against the flapping doors as I washed the last knife.

I was rinsing out the sink when the back door opened behind me. There was silence. I turned to see PopPop standing there with the door open, his face as white and colorless as a winter sky.

"Pop?" I turned off the water and dried my hands, moving towards him. "Pop? You all right?"

He trembled as he spoke. "Have you been in the playhouse lately?"

"No. Not since the fall. Why? PopPop, what's wrong?"

He turned and the storm door slammed behind him. "Come on out here a minute," he said.

I grabbed my sweater from a hook by the back door and ran after him. The door to the playhouse was wide open. The vacuum cleaner was tumbled around the door. PopPop stepped over it all and disappeared inside. I followed him.

And stopped short. "Oh, no!" I couldn't believe it. PopPop was kneeling on one knee in the corner staring openmouthed above him. Every piece of furniture, everything that had been in the main room of the playhouse had been turned upside down and jammed into the ceiling. The table hung by its legs from the broken plasterboard, the chairs dangled from two or three legs, the cradle drooped from one rocker, the broom jutted out of the corner, and a doll was suspended in the air, its hand pushed through the ceiling.

54

Everywhere there was dust, broken plaster, and turmoil. The only order was that everything was exactly as it had always been, only upside down. Driven into the ceiling.

"How did this happen?" I asked.

PopPop looked at me. "You don't know anything about this?"

"PopPop! How could I? How could this happen?"

He rubbed his hand across his chin and cheeks, making them scrape and scratch. "Must be vandals," he answered. "Sure is the strangest thing I've ever seen. Call your grandmother."

I backed out of the playhouse and started towards the house. I ran. I could see myself running as if I were an observer. Here's Zoe running to tell her grandmother, I thought. Here's Zoe acting amazed. But I wasn't. I knew how this had happened. It was as clear as if Zoe Louise herself had left her signature.

Grandma gaped up at the ceiling. "Joe! How could this have happened? *When* could this have happened? We're always home. There's always somebody here. Wouldn't we have heard this?"

"I don't know. I don't know," he answered. He reached up and tugged at one of the chairs. It resisted. "Think we should call Sheriff Towney?"

Grandma shrugged. "What could *he* do?"

"You're right. This may have been like this since —

When did you say you were out here last, Zoe?"

"Right before Thanksgiving," I whispered. "Right before it got real cold, that snow."

PopPop grabbed the chair with two hands then and gave a hard yank. It came loose, showering his hair with plaster. "Whoever did this was pretty strong," he said. Then he pulled the table down, the other chair. The rocker fell on its own. The doll needed to be hammered around its hand until it was freed. The room was destroyed. The furniture, now right-sided and released, was lopsided and bent. The ceiling trickled chunks and dust.

"What'll we do?" I asked PopPop.

He brushed the dust off his arms and sighed. "Well, I gotta get the truck to the dump before it gets dark. This is going to be a bigger project than I originally thought." He looked at me thoughtfully. "Are you sure you're going to use this place this year?" he asked.

I shrugged. "I guess," I told him. Past his shoulder, in the tiny bedroom I could see the furniture in there was still all right. I could see the small bed pushed against the wall. I could see Zoe Louise sitting there. Her arms were crossed and her small stockinged foot was tapping nervously on the bare wood floor.

"Come with me to the dump, Zoe. I'm gonna need a hand," PopPop said, and he left the playhouse.

Grandma began sweeping up, moving the chairs and gathering all the broken plaster into a pile. I looked in at Zoe Louise. She ran her arm across her nose and then rested her sad face on her fist.

"Wait here," I said softly. "I'll be back." I held up my open hand to Zoe Louise in promise.

Grandma answered. "Well, I'll sweep some of this up, but then I have to get back inside and start dinner."

I ran across the yard to PopPop, who was starting up the truck, and without thinking, when I saw the small, brown leather shoes on the old winter grass, I scooped them up and put them in my sweater pockets. Oh, Zoe Louise, I thought, what is the matter with you? What next? What next?

With one thing and another I didn't get back to the playhouse till after dinner, till it was dark. Once inside I found the little lamp didn't work, but the tiny bedroom glowed with the sound of Zoe Louise's soft breath. She was curled up on the bed, sleeping, and it was as though the room had a dying fire in it and was lit by the dimmest smudge.

"Zoe Louise," I whispered, and she stirred as I sat on the edge of the bed. I slipped my sneakers off, and climbed onto the bed beside her. Gently I drew the strands of dirty hair away from her gray face, tucking them behind her ear. I was surprised to see I had grown bigger than she was. I had passed her.

She sighed and then sat up suddenly, happy to see me. "Zoe! You must come! Papa will be here any minute with my pony! Momma says! And he's bringing a saddle and bright-red leather reins. You have to be there. I want you there."

"Why'd you do that?" I asked, pointing with my chin to the main room, through the archway.

"Do what?" she asked.

"The furniture. Everything upside down. Broken."

She scratched her head, yawned. "I couldn't find you. I waited and waited, and I thought maybe the furniture was wrong, that something had been moved and you wouldn't come back unless I got it right, so I tried it all different ways, and I thought maybe it was all upside down, and I fixed it, and sure enough, here you are." She smiled. And as she did, a clump of her hair fell from her head onto her lap. She didn't seem to notice. She went on smiling at me. I felt my heart begin to break and looked away.

Her hand slipped into mine then, like a tiny ebbing current in a river feeling its way, and I looked at her. Our eyes locked and this time I did not look away. And then as if my mind were an old book and I would find the right place for her to read, I thumbed through my thoughts until I stood at the place in the woods with my mother by the memory roses. I could feel the stickers prick my legs. I could hear my mother's voice talking about the little girl who had died. The little girl who had my name. It took a long time, as long as it takes the moon to move across a window pane, but when Zoe Louise finally looked away and stood up, I felt like I had been sitting there for years.

"So," she said, "now we know."

I was silent.

"How'd she die? This little rosebush girl?" she asked with a coldness that made me uneasy.

I shrugged and chewed on my fingernail. The room was growing chilly.

"Well, you'd better find out," she said matter-of-factly, and then she seemed to shake herself, shedding the gloom that had settled on us. "Come on, Zoe. Come up the stairs. See my pony. My birthday cake. Papa's coming." She was looking under the bed. "Where are my shoes?"

I began to reach into my pocket when she laughingly held my sneakers in the air. "I'll wear yours!" And before I knew it she had slipped my sneakers over her torn, faded socks, and with the laces flapping she ran from the room. I felt sad. I felt I was losing my Zoe Louise, that she was a spring bouquet that was wilting and drying before my eyes. Let her have my sneakers, I thought, touching her scuffed-up shoes in my pockets. But suddenly something awful began to happen.

There was an awful tightness, a cold grip around my ankles. Something had seized my feet. And my feet began walking motions even though I sat on the edge of the bed. My feet scraped back and forth on the bare wood floor. I couldn't make them stop. They began to run, my feet at the ends of my legs, like strangers to me, and I clung to the edge of the bed, fighting them, wanting to scream. But they were strong, determined. I was dragged off the bed, across the room, pulling the old mattress with me. My feet were running, running. I grabbed the doorway from the bedroom and managed against a torrent of pressure to stand up on my feet, and then there was no stopping them. I tried to grab things, to stop myself—the broken table, the door, the little banister into the house, the tree branch, anything—but they tore across the lawn. I could feel the grass under them. The cold ground. They bounded up the back stairs to the big house and stopped.

Breathless, I stopped. It was over. I just stood there and started to cry. Where was Grandma? Pop-Pop? Then, whiplike and fierce, my feet began kicking the door. My stocking feet began kicking the door as if to knock it down. And then they stopped.

Waited, and began again. Only to stop once more. This time I opened the door, pain streaking from my toes up my calves, and as soon as the door was open my feet ran across the kitchen floor, directly to the back-staircase door.

"No," I whispered. "No."

My feet waited. I dared not refuse to open the door this time. I could see bloody spots spreading wider on my white socks. The door opened easily and inside the stairway was streaked with sunlight even though the windows in the kitchen were dark. The door at the top was wide open.

"Hurry!" I heard her call. "What's taking you?"

Zoe Louise was standing at the top, my sneakers on her feet. Without my consent, my feet ran up the stone steps, two at a time, slipping on loose slates, stubbing my toes against broken mortar, until I was standing in the hallway, bathed in light, and the door slammed behind me.

Gasping for breath, crying, trembling, I shouted at her. "Don't you ever, ever do anything like that to me again!"

She faced me squarely and pouted. It was as if she had just noticed how upset I was. And how I had gotten there. She placed her hand on my shoulder. "I'm sorry," she said. "Really I am. But I wanted you to come."

It was then that I noticed. Her face was soft

and rosy, her dress was crisp and clean as if it had just been ironed, and her hair—only moments ago falling out in sad clumps—shone in the sunlight. My Zoe Louise. More solid and real than she had ever been. I breathed deeply, quieting my sobs and feeling inexplicably safe. I looked around me, at the unfamiliar pictures on my grandmother's walls, the pretty cotton runner that covered the main steps to downstairs. There was still the sweet aroma of melting chocolate everywhere.

Zoe Louise reached for my hand and frowned when she couldn't hold it. I looked down at my hand, then held it up to the brightly curtained window and watched the shadows of my skeleton wiggle beneath the flesh.

"Come," she said. "Hold my hand."

When I concentrated on my hand and on her hand I seemed to grow solid there, and then our fingers intertwined and her hand squeezed mine.

"Wait," I said. I waved my other hand over her head, around her head, and through her head. Then I concentrated on my fingers, sent myself to their tips, and watched them touch the bow in her hair.

"You've got it," she said, tugging at me. "Let's see if Papa's here." And I followed her down the main staircase into the waiting cloud of melting chocolate.

The kitchen was a bustle of activity, with pans all over the counters, and on the table next to a heavy pink oil lamp was a basket loaded with eggs and a cloth sack overflowing with flour. Steam rose from a black stove where Grandma's shiny white one normally was, and a short, older woman stood at this black stove stirring something with a long wooden spoon. A younger woman, who I knew to be Zoe Louise's mother, was opening an oven and rearranging things inside that were baking. I saw her look up at Zoe Louise, smile, and turn back to her pans. She held the hot pan with a cloth, but gingerly moved the steaming pastries around with her fingers. Without looking up again, she called out, "Stay clean, sweetheart. Papa will be home in a little while."

She didn't notice me, didn't do a double take to see who this strange child was in her kitchen. She didn't look at me, didn't see me. Zoe Louise didn't even stop, but slammed out of the back screen door, a door with carvings and designs I had never seen before with screening nailed neatly to the back.

My hand passed through its doorknob, and remembering, I cautiously stepped through it out onto the back steps. The steps that PopPop painted gray every spring, but were now a rich, shiny green. And the light and the air were shimmery, like I had never seen before, except maybe through the curtains upstairs. It was as if I moved through the thinnest mist that made everything shine and glimmer. I squeezed my eyes closed, blinked, but the light remained the same. It was lovely. The colors of the flowers were intense and rich, and I could distinguish the delicate aroma of each one by just looking at them.

Zoe Louise had run ahead of me, and before I could catch up, a little boy had silently fallen into step behind her. His long straight hair formed a halo around his head, but in his hands, clasped behind his back, I could see the stiff legs of a dead bird. "Birthday girl, hey, birthday girl, where are your shoes?" he called softly and when Zoe Louise turned to him, he slowed his pace. Zoe Louise looked at him and then at me. She smiled, standing there in my sneakers.

"He's got a dead bird in his hands," I told her.

She stood stone still and watched him like a cat would watch a piece of string trailing across the rug. "I'll bet you a silver dollar you have a dead bird there," she said to him.

He stopped short and I watched his fingers open and the bird fall out onto the grass. "Do not," he said.

"Bet him it's in his pocket," I said, and concentrating on my fingers, I lifted the dead bird from the grass and slipped it into the wide pocket of his short pants.

"In your pocket," she said. "You owe me a silver dollar."

"I do not," he insisted.

"Do too."

"Do not."

"Why don't you look?"

With that he reached deep into both pockets and in one yank pulled them both inside out. He stared at the dead bird that fell stiffly at his feet. "How'd you do that?"

"Oliver, when are you going to learn I have powers? I know everything you do and everywhere you go, and if you are not nice to me, I'm going to slice off your head and stuff it in your pocket."

She pointed her nose in the air and walked off into the woods . . . only I suddenly noticed it wasn't the woods at all. It was a garden, a most beautiful garden that extended farther back than I had ever seen, and beyond the garden were fields and rolling hills, not a house to be seen, not a road, not a highway. Beyond the farthest hill I could see the lighthouse, a white one with a red cap. I stood stunned as Oliver turned and ran towards me and through me, and I could feel the hot breeze of him suck away my breath for an instant.

"That was the one and only Oliver," Zoe Louise called over her shoulder.

"This is so beautiful, Zoe Louise," I sighed. "So beautiful. I can't believe this is Grandma's garden. That this is the same place."

"It's *my* garden," she said. "Come on, come see."

I turned back to the house, to Grandma's house in time to see Oliver bound up the back steps and in the door. Yes, it was almost exactly as my grandmother's, with the same windows, the same back steps painted a different color, the same slope to the roof, the identical chimney. Only different. The trees were different, shading the other side of the house. There was a line of small lilacs where Grandma had a big pine. A birdbath where PopPop grew his peonies.

"Zoe!" she demanded. "Come. Before Papa gets home and I don't have any more time for you."

I followed her deeper into the property, filled with wonder, a wonder I have not felt again in my life. The outlines of everything were as clear as sliced glass, the ground was like air beneath me, I could look right at the sun and see a swirling blackness within its light. I wanted to lie on my back on the grass and seep into the soil, melt into the earth, but Zoe Louise was standing boldly before me.

"Concentrate on your mouth," she said.

"What—"

"Just concentrate on making your mouth there. Like I do when your grandmother brings us cherries."

She stared at my lips, a fat raspberry held in her lifted fingers. "Do it," she demanded.

I concentrated on my mouth, touched the parted lips with my tongue, my fingers, felt the teeth, pouted, bit my lips, felt them grow dense and firm and she popped the ripe berry into my mouth. As clear as the air seemed, the taste of that raspberry was as equally pure. It was tangy and sweet, and made my lips pucker and the backs of my ears crinkle. The berry's little black hairs gathered on my tongue and I swallowed.

"Want more?"

I nodded. I followed her back into the garden, and there—where I knew the stand of rosebushes to be—was a thick row of raspberry shrubs, with tons and tons of berries fattening in the sun. Partying birds flew in and out of them, and if I concentrated

67

on my fingers and the backs of my hands and the palms, I could pluck berries off their prickly stems easily. But unless I concentrated on my lips as well, the berries would fall to the grass when I went to eat them.

There was a soft noise behind me that I heard for a long time, like the slow ticking of a clock, but I didn't turn to see, I just let it come—*swish*, *click*, *swish*, *click*—until Zoe Louise's mother was standing beside me, almost in me, her small empty bucket passing through my arm.

"Berries ripe today, dear?" she asked.

Zoe Louise swung around startled. She hadn't heard the footsteps. "Oh, Momma! You frightened me!"

I watched the beautiful woman as she approached my friend and drew her close. She put her arm around her daughter and cradled the child's head in the crook of her neck. "I was watching you," she said, almost sadly, "seeing you and how big you're getting. Eleven. I can hardly believe it."

I watched as Zoe Louise turned towards her mother, passed her arms around her mother's waist, and nestled her chin in the woman's neck. They stood there like that in a hug. I had seen only statues do that, stay together so long. And it had been a long time since I had snuggled on Grandma's lap. Zoe Louise seemed to have forgotten I was there. Then her mother patted her, smoothed back her hair, and puffed up her bright bows. "Let's get some berries," she said, "for dessert tonight, in case anyone would rather have fruit and cream than cake."

"But these are my berries," Zoe Louise said, turning to the rows of bushes.

"Now, Zoe Louise, this is not your personal berry collection. You know Alethea uses them for bread and jams, and sometimes we like a little juice—"

"But I never want anybody to eat any more of my berries once I have my birthday. I even want the birds kept away. That's what I want for my birthday—these bushes."

"Instead of a pony?" her mother asked, humoring her. I could tell her mother didn't take her as seriously as I did and I paid close attention. I drew close to where they were and watched.

Zoe Louise laughed at herself. Softened. "For me and my pony, that's who the berries will be for. And no one else will ever be allowed to touch them, or they will regret it the rest of their lives."

The woman laughed gently and turned to the bushes. She began dropping fat berry after fat berry into her bucket. "Oh, Zoe Louise LaBarge, you should have been born a princess. With ladies-in-waiting, and coachmen—"

"And ponies!"

69

"And ponies." Zoe Louise's mother drew close to where I was standing and I froze. I didn't move, watching so close as she selected the fattest berries, the darkest ones, watching her arm pass through my shoulder, her hair brush against my face, her skirt press into my legs. I smelled her perfume like I had smelled the flowers, clear and sharp. We stood superimposed on each other and I didn't dare move. I felt her warmth engulf me like the warmest winter fire, till my cheeks grew flushed. She held still and looked down into her bucket, measuring, thinking. I could no longer contain myself. The remembered sight of the long hug was taunting, tempting like the smell of melting chocolate in the air. As slowly and as gently as I could, I slipped my arms around her waist and rested my cheek on her shoulder. We were very still. I didn't breathe, then opening my eyes I saw Zoe Louise standing there, staring at me.

"That's *my* mother," she said.

Her mother glanced up from her bucket. "*My* mother, *my* berries, *my* pony, *my, my, my.*"

Ashamed and embarrassed I ducked out of the circle of this woman's heart and backed away. I couldn't meet Zoe Louise's eyes, but I could feel her turn back to her berry picking and then after a moment, her small hand was on my shoulder and her hand held out a berry to my lips.

"Zoe Louise!" her mother suddenly said. "Why haven't you your shoes on out here? For goodness' sakes, you know you're not to go out in just your stockings. Alethea doesn't need more darning to do."

I looked down then at Zoe Louise's feet and saw them in my sneakers. The laces were stained with berry juice. Her brown leather shoes weighed my pockets down. But just then, just then, just then, it was awful.

I couldn't shake it.

I couldn't stop it.

I heard Grandma's voice. "Zoe! Zoe!"

Calling, calling me, from the top of the stairs, from the yard, from her room. A heaviness seized me that threatened to pound me into the ground. I had to go. Had to get home. Grandma. My home. I turned and ran towards the house, towards the stairs that I hoped would take me back.

8

I f l e w unnoticed past Alethea, who was leaning over the porcelain sink. The door at the foot of the back staircase was wide open and a basket of fresh, fragrant sheets and towels was sitting there, waiting to be brought up. It tipped and spilled beneath my feet as I stumbled past, fighting against waves of time that held me back in a frightful current. My legs were heavy, too slow, and the staircase loomed above me like a treacherous cliff. "Coming, Gram," I tried to call, but my voice lay like thick cotton at the back of my throat. No words passed my lips. Even my breath was thick honey.

"Zoe! Zoe!" It was Grandma looking for me, calling. But it was also Zoe Louise coming after me, trying to stop me, trying to keep me from

Grandma. But no, Zoe Louise was right beside me, and she was trying to tell me something.

"Wait," she was saying, standing there in her fresh cotton dress, her fingers still stained with raspberries. She was holding out my sneakers to me. And she was saying something, something about the staircase, something about going up the staircase, that it was too hard—

But I was gripped with a panic that was bigger than her reasoning, stronger than any current, and I wouldn't listen to her. I clawed my way up, a step at a time, the soul of the world pushing me down. "Zoe! Zoe, my shoes," I could hear her call to me, but I didn't care about her shoes. I didn't care if she ever saw her shoes again, even though they weighed like boulders in my pockets.

I was more than halfway up the cliff of stairs, against a soundless wind, losing the light that had been so precious, suddenly aware that Zoe Louise was clinging to me, begging me, and when I turned to look at her, I was stunned to see she had wrapped her arms around my legs and her head was even with my hip, two drowning creatures we were. I could see the skin of her head through her rotting hair, and through that the plate of her skull, and through that the pale, watery blood soaking through her brain. She turned her face up to me, her beautiful Zoe Louise face, and as she did, a fragment of her parchment cheek tore from her face and stuck to my shirt. Her eyes turned up to mine, her dry, transparent eyes with the barest flicker of life, her awful eyes held to her face with the thinnest cobwebs of lids. "Come back," she whispered, and behind her dry, cracked lips were gray and terrible small teeth.

A current of the most awful fear surged through me. The hair stood up all over my body—my arms, the back of my neck, my calves, and a scream finally broke out of my throat. In one swift, powerful motion, I threw her from me, pushed her away, and out, and off, with my arms and my legs kicking. And I watched in horror as her small body flew from me, flew straight across the expanse of the stairs to the wall above the bottom door. She hit the wall and tumbled like a sack full of croquet mallets in a heap below on the spilled towels and sheets.

An awful silence. My breath was coming in gasps. I was trembling so hard my elbows were knocking against the wall. The only noises. I listened for her. She lay at the bottom, motionless. Was she dead? Would this be the way Zoe Louise would finally die? I listened for her mother. Her mother would find her there like that, her fingers still stained from raspberries.

"Zoe Louise?" I whispered. "Zo."

She stirred, like a wounded squirrel in a pile of autumn leaves. Her bones rattled. Her dry skin rustled. Her hand rose, clutching my sneakers. "Please," she rasped. "Give me my shoes. You can't take them up with you this way."

I stared at my sneakers in her hand. And felt in my pockets for her shoes. The wind, the roaring in the stairs had stopped. I inched down a couple of steps towards her. I put her shoes on a middle step. "Here. Get them yourself." And I clambered back up to the top, exhausted.

She said a soft "oh," and her hand fell with my sneakers.

"And keep the old sneakers," I told her. "I don't want them." And at that I turned to open the top door and let myself out into my grandmother's house. But the roaring started again, softly, not enough to push me down the stairs, but enough so I couldn't lift my arm to open the door. I'd thought it was over. Done. I started to cry.

"Zoe!" she suddenly screamed in the enclosed staircase, and my name resounded and reverberated all over, to the marrow of my bones. I clamped my hands over my ears till the roaring stopped. "Help me," I heard her say as she reached for her shoes.

I could move my arm in her direction, but not in the direction of the door. I could move my feet down, towards her, but not up. Not up. And so, trapped, my heart gone beyond fear to complete surrender, I eased myself down the stairs, sliding from step to step, groping my way towards her, picking up her small leather shoes and feeling them in my hands like stones that would bring me to the bottom of a murky pond. As I drew closer, she pulled herself up. Her dress hung in tatters from her bony shoulders. She watched me. Her voice was raspy and weak. "My shoes. Put them on me," she said. She held out a small foot. The shoes had a warm and dusty feeling. I held them out.

"On," she said again.

Gently then, not wanting to touch her, I slipped one shoe on her foot. Her gray sock fell away like dust to the touch, but she sighed, and held out her other foot. The second shoe slipped on easily and then her hands were there with mine, buttoning them, securing them. Her hands flushed pink as she buttoned, blood coursing into the wings of a butterfly as it struggles to break its cocoon. Both buttoned, she rubbed her eyes roughly, her skin reddening, her strong eyes opening to stare at me.

"You don't listen," she scolded with returning strength. "It's too hard to go back to your house this way, going *up* the stairs, don't you remember? Especially when you're carrying something. You have to go *down* the stairs from the upstairs hall to go home." Her tattered clothes weren't tattered anymore. My own fingers were becoming pale memories.

"But you brought my sneakers here with you," I said, my voice returning weakly. "You've brought dolls, pencils, oranges. Lots of things. A lot of times."

Zoe Louise shrugged, stood up, and smoothed down her skirt. She turned the basket over and piled the towels and the sheets back in. "I know," she answered angrily. "And you're right, it doesn't make sense. It has something to do with the direction of the stairs. It's just too hard when you come in from the bottom here."

"It doesn't make any sense."

She glared at me. "When does time ever make sense? Sometimes when I come down the stairs to find you, you are a little girl. Sometimes you are older, bigger than I am, and I even came looking for you once and you were grown, a woman, and you didn't see me at all."

"How can that be?"

Then like two bows drawn over vibrating strings in perfect harmonies, our names were sung simultaneously and echoed in the enclosed staircase.

"Zoe."

"Zoe Louise."

"Momma's calling," she said, and like always she turned, stepped through the bottom doorway, and was instantly gone, leaving me alone. I sat staring at the basket until Grandma called again. Then feeling like I was just getting up after a long sickness, I lifted my heavy sneaker, slipped my nearly transparent foot into it, and laced it up. Then the other. I stood, but it felt as if an unforgiving gravity was holding me down. I backed down the stairs, eased my way past the basket of laundry, and without looking anymore, without worrying if I'd be seen, I passed through the door, through the busy kitchen and the brightly lit living room, up the main staircase to the hall, where I slipped through the top stairway door, and thundered down the steps easily. The winds and currents of time no longer fought me. The door at the bottom swung open to my grandmother's call. Her African violets were waiting in the window.

"Gram?"

My grandmother was sitting in her chair in the living room, her crocheting in her lap.

"Did you call?"

She looked up at me, a faraway look in her eyes. "Why, yes, I called you before. Now what was it I wanted?"

"Didn't you call me just now?"

"No. Before— Oh, I know what I wanted. PopPop and I were wondering where the old Scrabble game was. Do you know?"

"Wasn't it down in the cellar? Maybe in the storage closet?"

"Hmmm, that sounds very possible." She sighed. "Why don't you see if you can find it. PopPop just went out for some ice cream. We'll have a game tonight."

"You mean you didn't call me a hundred times, right up to just a few minutes ago?"

She looked at me strangely. "I called you once. Why didn't you answer if you thought I called you a hundred times?"

I leaned into her chair and fiddled with the buttons on my shirt. "Well, not a hundred—"

"Whatever. Go on. See if you can find the Scrabble box."

"But it's so dark down in the cellar at night. It's spooky."

"Take the flashlight," she said.

I guess I was staring at her.

"What is it, Zoe?"

"I feel scared."

She looked at me blankly. "Of the cellar?"

I shrugged. "Can I sit in your lap, Grandma? You know. Like I used to?"

She moved her crocheting aside, watching me carefully. "Of course you can. If you still fit."

I moved in front of her, sat across her legs, and put my arms around her neck. Where my cheek used to nuzzle against her soft chest, now my face was even with hers. I was all elbows and knees, and she winced in pain when my behind bones dug into her legs.

"Maybe I should sit in *your* lap," she offered, and she hugged me close. But it wasn't the same. I tried to let myself melt into her arms, tried to feel the old feeling—safe from echoing bathrooms, dark cellars, and mysterious staircases—and even though she stroked my hair like she used to, tucking strands behind my ear, it wasn't the same anymore. It didn't make me safe.

Oscar came and tried to jump up beside us. He made a couple of false attempts, half starts, and we laughed at him. I slid off Grandma's lap and lifted his fat old body onto her lap where he fit easily. He would have smiled if he could have. I knelt on the floor at Grandma's feet and buried my face in his fur. He pressed his flattened face against my neck and snorted.

"Oh, Oscar," Grandma sighed, "time's taking its toll on you, my fat boy."

"On me, too, Gram," I admitted, surprising even myself.

She looked at me then, her eyes smiling, her mouth trying not to. "Indeed it is," she said. "I thought I spied a gray hair or two on your wise old head." She tousled my hair. "Go on now. See if you can find the game before PopPop gets back."

A bare light bulb hung from a beam in the center of the basement, where it was cool and damp, and in the corner was a huge black furnace that would click once in a while and it sounded like it held an ocean of softly boiling water. I could hear Grandma's footsteps above me in the living room. "In the storage closet?" I shouted at the ceiling.

"Should be," I heard her muffled answer, close by. "With the Chinese checkers and the dominoes."

The storage closet loomed on the opposite wall, its two doors painted white, turned sooty. They creaked open at my touch, and I thought I heard a little mouse scamper away in one of the bottom shelves. I shivered and hugged myself, not wanting to touch anything. There were boxes marked "Loretta's crystal" and "Jessie's artwork" and on one shelf, atop a pile of newspapers, were some games, Scrabble on top. I slid it off the shelf, holding it by its edges, and trying not to disturb the dust and grime. I listened for mice.

"Find it?" Grandma called. Oscar cried from the top of the steps, afraid to come down.

"Yes," I answered. I blew the dust off the box and saw the newspapers then, their decorative headlines and yellowed pages. *The Island Star.* I looked closer. *December 16, 1869.* I placed the Scrabble game at my feet and eased the paper from the

81

shelf. *Prentice family hosts gala holiday reception* — I went and stood beneath the light bulb — *for Grace Evangelical Church members. Festive decorations, holiday music supplied by the Grace Melody Choir, and a magnificent assortment of food were enjoyed by all.*

Oscar worried and whined at the head of the stairs.

"Hush!" I told him, going back to the closet. I pulled out more papers. There were hundreds. Some were brittle and crumbled to my touch. Others seemed damp and moldy. I picked out a few and put them on top of the Scrabble box. They were not in any order, dated 1872, 1869, 1865.

Oscar was pacing back and forth and Grandma was in the kitchen. "Look what I found, Grandma."

"Oh, what deadly old thing could you have possibly found down there?" she asked. I placed the papers and the game on the kitchen table, and she peered over my shoulder.

"Old newspapers," I told her. "Real old newspapers, from the 1800s."

"Hunh," she said. "Those were here when we moved in. We should have thrown them out long ago."

"Whose papers are these?" I asked. "The people before you?"

She thought a minute. "Well, let's see. We bought this house from the Sturms. They weren't here in the 1800s though. And it was the Clavenshires before that, and there might have been more, but I remember hearing the house was originally built by a LaVarr or LaBarge, or something like that. Maybe these belong to them."

She noticed me shudder and rubbed my arms. "You should put a sweater on to go down in the cellar."

"Do you know much about the history of this house? About what happened here before us?"

"No, not really. It would be interesting to find something though, wouldn't it?" She leafed through some brittle pages. *"January 3, 1869,"* she read. *"Town council holds hearings for the back road to be built along the steep bluffs overlooking the bay."*

"Is that Bluff Drive?" I asked.

"Must be." She dropped the paper on the kitchen table. "If I start reading these, I'll never stop. You read them and if you find anything at all about this house or this road out here, come let us know. I hear PopPop's truck. Come on, you get the ice cream bowls and I'll dust off the Scrabble."

The newspapers sat on the kitchen table all night while we played Scrabble in the dining room. And the whole while I was looking for three-letter words that used a *q* and places to put my five *o*'s, I was wondering what years it had been that Zoe Louise lived here. When had she eaten raspberries in Grand-

83

ma's yard, and when, exactly, had her father brought her the pony? I remembered how in the playhouse she had told me I'd better find out how the girl with the rosebushes died. Tomorrow I'd read through the old newspapers. And maybe I'd find the story of a death, the death of an eleven-year-old girl.

9

That night, with the moon shining through my window like a taunting beacon, I tossed in bed. My legs tangled in the quilt. The pillow was like a sack of birdseed under my head.

I couldn't sleep. I felt as though there were a light switch inside me that would let me sleep if only I could find it and gently turn it off. But thoughts of Zoe Louise kept me hovering over the bed, open-eyed, restless, and stiff. I put my head where the moonbeams shone across my sheet and stared up into the moon.

Even Oscar took a long time to settle down. He held his head up and watched me warily. He waited for me to grow still and I kept him waiting. Finally, he rested his chin on my knee and began to snore. His snoring had always made Zoe Louise laugh. She would press her hand to her nose to flatten her face like his, and she would tumble over onto her side in a fit of laughter. Until she woke him. Then she would be nervously, giddily quiet. Until he slept and snored and she would begin again.

Now in the dark, I stroked the soft wrinkles on his brow and thought of the staircase. If I were very careful to take nothing with me and bring nothing back, and start at the bottom from this side, and the top from the other, I could probably travel the staircase easily on my own. Step back into the past. See Zoe Louise and find out what year she was living in. I wondered if she had gotten her pony yet. I wondered if she were still alive. I thought of the staircase. I could almost smell the chocolate. Maybe the laundry would still be stacked at the bottom of the stairs, if Alethea had been too busy with the party to put it away.

Slowly I slipped from beneath the twisted quilt. I eased Oscar's head onto the pillow and he continued to snore. My robe was beside my bed on the floor and I carefully stepped into it, drew it over my arms and about my shoulders, and zipped it up. The clock in the downstairs hall bonged twice.

I would boil some water, make a mug of sleepy tea, and maybe read through some of the newspapers. I opened my door into the hall. It was dark and peaceful and my footsteps didn't make a sound as I went down the main staircase to the kitchen.

I filled the teapot with water and set it over a blue flame. Then I sat at the table and drew the newspapers towards me. They smelled damp and old, and mysterious. Out of the corner of my eye I could see that the back-staircase door was opened the slightest bit. I read a couple of headlines. I thought of looking at the obituaries, but I couldn't. It was too dark in the house. Too late. I would just make some tea and bring it into the living room to drink in the darkness. Or maybe I'd put on the light and read a magazine.

I got up to find a tea bag and a mug and found myself standing before the door to the back staircase. I touched the doorknob tenderly and the door opened at my touch. Then in the distance, even though the moon was shining bright as could be there in the kitchen, I could hear rain, a monotonous, pound-ing rain.

I stepped into the stairwell and looked up. The top door was open and a gray light filtered in along the walls. I dared not call out. I would wake Grandma and PopPop. I closed the door tight behind me.

"Zoe Louise?" I whispered, forgetting my tea.

But there was only the sound of rain. And some-thing else, something soft and repetitive. "Zo?" I whispered again. I started up the staircase in the darkness. It felt like I was rising into a grayness of early dawn. My hands trailed along the walls, and my feet made no sound. I was silent. There was only rain, and now I recognized the sound of the quietest, most mournful weeping.

My feet reached the top of the stairs and the stone slab there was damp and cool. There was no smell of chocolate now, but strangely the sharp smell of a forgotten wood fire that had burnt into ash. Thinking of my hand, making my hand whole and solid, I touched the top door and slowly pushed it all the way open. It was early dawn here. The rain pounded right outside the hall window, and the summer leaves of the tree through the hall windows were slick and shining.

I followed the sound of the weeping to a doorway that opened into a dark room, my grandmother's room, but not. A shadow hung in the corner and as my eyes adjusted to the dim light, I saw a long, heavy black dress hanging from a brass hanger against the wall. The dress looked fussed over, its ruffles and folds perfectly arranged, its lace collar turned carefully, and its sleeves stuffed with paper that showed at its cuffs.

It was a black dress, a funeral dress. I stepped soundlessly into the room and turned towards the sorrowful sounds by the windows. A woman was sitting there in a soft chair, staring out into the rain. Her hair covered her face, and she was crying—an endless, boundless crying that just went on and on and on, with no variation, no wailing, no sniffling, just a weeping like the ocean pounds, like a mother breathes when her child is dead.

A man's voice spoke to her in the darkness. "Please, Cornelia, come to bed."

"I can't sleep," she answered, and she wiped her long fingers slowly across her cheeks, and then along the nightgown covering her legs. A wind gusted and somewhere in the house a shutter banged. "Oh, Zoe Louise . . ." she said, almost silently.

I felt tears streaming over my own cheeks. I was too late. It was over. Was there anything I could have done? Any way I could have changed things? I drew close to Zoe Louise's mother and settled around her feet. Then, as quiet as smoke, I rested my head on her knee for a long, long time, and I listened to the rain, to the wind, to her sad crying until the room grew lighter and the man finally came and led her to bed.

When I returned home to my grandmother's house, the water in the teapot was just beginning to boil.

There was no one to speak to, no one to tell that my oldest friend had died, that I had seen her mother's funeral clothes, and that I had felt an emptiness that I thought would swallow me up. There was nothing more I could do. Not allowing for quirks of time and the mysterious interwoven waves of order and disorder. I was sure it was all over.

When I got back to bed that night I drew Oscar under the covers with me. He snuggled close, as limp and pliant as a stuffed bear, and in the darkness I knew I had to tell him that Zoe Louise was finally dead. I knew he wouldn't understand, but he was the only one I could tell, the only one who had ever seen her.

I tested him. "Where's PopPop?" I said softly. His head bolted up and he looked expectantly towards the door. I calmed him, patted him, until he lay back down. "PopPop's sleeping," I cooed. "Don't worry." Then I watched as I asked him, "Where's Zoe Louise?" Again he sat up and whimpered, his tail flicking back and forth.

"Oh, shh, shhh," I said, hugging him to me. "She's dead now. Zoe Louise is gone. Shh, shh." And he settled down again, resting his chin in the crook of my neck. A terrible uneasiness covered me. Part of me said it no longer mattered how Zoe Louise had died, how an eleven-year-old child had died over a hundred years ago. But there was another part that was telling me it wasn't too late at all. That there might still be time.

In the morning I would read those old newspapers. There were hundreds of them, but as sleep started to come and soften all the sharp edges to things, I slowly realized where I could easily find the year of Zoe's death. I fell asleep dreaming about what I would do in the morning. And I think that was one of those nights when I would wake to find twigs and bits of grass in my sheets.

Morning came and my bike sped along the smooth backroads of the island towards the cemetery. All the towering trees and roadside shrubs had taken on a pale blue-green haze in the early light. I'd worn my jacket but didn't zip it and the cool, damp air crept over my chest. I could feel spring coming all over my body. But there was no joy in it. It only reminded me of the wind that made no sound, that force that had pressed me into the steps and kept me down. I felt uneasy and troubled.

I tried not to think about it, but concentrated instead on my pedaling, the loose gears, the hill that gently crested by the churchyard. The cemetery. When I approached the drive I made a wide arc and bumped over the entrance brickwork and entered into a strange morning silence. I had never been here without my mother before. The sun was a few inches above rising and its pale light outlined the old cedars against the sky. The tombstones, all tilting slightly with the press of the earth, were waiting for me.

I left my bike where the grass began and walked slowly among them. Past the double stone of Caleb and Sally Havens, past stone angels and marble slabs, until I stood before the one I had come to see. Zoe, was all it said. I knelt before her stone, ran my fingers over the three letters, and traced the words *Louise LaBarge* where they could have been written. It would have fit. I tried to make out where the dates would have been carved beneath, but the crumblings were irregular, jagged. If there had been a date there, it hadn't left the barest trace. It was long gone. If only you could tell me, I thought. If only.

I got up and moved to the next stone, to see where the date was normally placed. I was jolted by what I read. Here was Cornelia LaBarge. Zoe Louise's mother? Born April 21, 1834. Went to heaven December 30, 1909. Quickly I calculated. Good. She died an old woman. I scanned the other stones. Jonathan LaBarge, surely her father. October 3, 1830–January 9, 1890. And here was Oliver La-Barge, without the dead bird in his pocket, 1865 to 1935, and his wife, Violet, and here his daughter, Louise. I felt as if someone had run an icy finger up my spine. They were all here. All proving how real this was. And everything was here except the date of Zoe Louise's death, and I was sure if I knew that, only knew that, I could prevent it. Take a tiny tuck in time, and she too could die an old woman with memories of a pony she once got on her eleventh birthday.

I looked again at Oliver's stone. Born 1865. That would mean Zoe Louise was probably born in 1859 or 1860, plus eleven, around 1870. That's when she would have died. It would have to be the newspapers around 1870 that I would search through.

Suddenly I was running from the cemetery. Pedaling away from the tombstones. Maybe there was still time.

The cellar was no lighter in the morning than it had been in the middle of the night, and the single bulb sent dark shadows into the storage closet. While Oscar whimpered at the top of the stairs, I shuffled through the papers, piling up all the ones I could find that had any dates from 1869 to 1871. My shirt and the insides of my arms were streaked and black. The pile was huge.

I took what I could carry and then quietly, so Grandma wouldn't hear me and want me to sit at the kitchen table with them, I stole up the stairs and through the backdoor. I hesitated at the top of the back steps and, holding the papers under one arm, I lifted Oscar under the other, to get him down the stairs and then, once in the grass, we ran together to the playhouse.

The door opened easily. I stepped inside, the hairs on the top of my head brushing along the ceiling, and I spread the papers out on the swept floor, while Oscar sniffed at the pile of crooked and broken furniture that was piled along one wall. I stood and looked at the spread newspapers. There were more down in the cellar, but this was a start.

I was halfway through the obituaries in the 1869 newspapers, when Oscar growled deep in his throat. He was staring at the door to the yard and the hair stood up all the way down his back.

Someone was there. Suddenly I grew cold and the hair stood up on my own arms. "It's okay, Oscar," I said, patting his back. I couldn't take my eyes from the door. I drew him close to me as a figure pushed right through. Nose, face, chest, arms, knees, legs. Slowly the figure materialized, like a trout suddenly visible on the floor of a river bed. Zoe Louise had never looked more terrible. It was hard to tell what was holding her together other than bits of shredded clothes and gristly tendons.

When Oscar saw who it was, he went to her gaily, oblivious of her condition, and ran a slow circle around her, his wagging tail making his rump rock left and right. She bent over to run her bony fingers over the top of his head, and when she did a thick runny fluid ran off her shoulders and throat and onto the floor at her feet. Then with tremendous effort, she straightened up and her lone remaining lusterless eye looked right at me. She came towards me, through the puddle she had made.

"I'm glad I found you," she said. "You must come with me."

An odd stench was beginning to fill the room. I thought of Grandma sniffing at the open refrigerator door, sniffing, fretting, "What is that? What is that?"

"No," I whispered. "Don't make me."

"What are you afraid of?" she asked. "The stairs will work for you, if you remember what to do."

"It's not the stairs," I said.

"Then what is it?" Her mouth still worked fine. If I had closed my eyes, I could have sworn it was the same Zoe Louise with a fresh dress and shining hair, and two eyes. But I dared not close my eyes. I backed away from her, wedged my back into the corner. I was trembling.

"It's you," I whispered. "You're awful."

She stamped her foot. A long thin bone tipped out from her ankle and fell on the floor with a rattle. It rolled away from her. "And whose fault is that?" she yelled. "You're no help!"

"But I think you're dead," I said. "I saw your mother. She was crying. And there was a black dress."

She slowly came closer to me and knelt in front

of me, her knees touching mine in that old, familiar position. I dared not close my eyes for even an instant. I stared at her wide-eyed and terrified. Her motions were loose-jointed and jerky like a puppet on a string, and she seemed to have trouble holding her head steady. I could sense her gathering all her strength to kneel before me. She lowered her head even with mine, her eyes with mine. I swallowed back salt that rose in my throat. At last I let her remaining eye take hold of mine. I didn't dare breathe.

As she wandered through my thoughts I felt myself again at her weeping mother's feet in the pale room at dawn. I felt the woman's soft nightgown against my cheek and saw the heavy black dress waiting on the wall. Quietly, quietly, from somewhere far away, I heard, "Cornelia, please, come to bed," and then I heard again the woman calling out to her dead child.

Zoe Louise sobbed once. A great intake of breath full of sorrow and unmentionable fear. "You must come," she begged me. "It's not too late."

But I didn't believe her. I didn't believe her rotting body that was falling apart like a doll left out in the rain all summer could even make it up the stairs again. She was dead. Zoe Louise was dead and she was a ghost and I wondered how long she would continue to haunt me.

"Come. Come," she was saying, her fingers winding around my upper arm, but I resisted and I was stronger. Her fingers passed through me. She pulled my hair, tugged at my shirt, kicked at my feet, but she went through me like wind through a willow tree. I barely felt it.

"It's too late!" I yelled at her. "Look at you! It's too late!"

She stood then, splattering blood and a clear oozing fluid all over me. Even though her face was only a skeleton's face, a child's skull, I could see the rage there, see the remaining flesh of a mouth stretched in a painful grimace of determination.

"Go home," I whispered from the corner. "Please go home, Zoe Louise."

She looked around the room then, and I thought she would wreck things, turn things over like she had once before, but her gaze settled on Oscar.

"No." I felt the word deep in my throat.

But she went right to him, and with more strength than I had thought she had, she scooped him up under her arm, kicked open the door with a suddenly powerful foot, and was gone.

"No! No! No!" I shouted. I ran after her, the stench of her rising from my clothes and my sticky chest and arms. I ran across the lawn to the house close behind her, like I had so many times before.

Only this time it wasn't a ghost in a party dress stealing my favorite doll. No, this time it was Zoe Louise. Rotting, dying, dripping, forlorn Zoe Louise, and she had my Oscar.

10

Time swirled and dodged around me. First I was in my grandmother's kitchen running after Zoe Louise, then I was in the kitchen of the past watching her disappear with Oscar out the back door. I was solid; I was transparent. Zoe Louise was a horrible pile of rotting flesh, then before I knew it she was a laughing girl running across the fresh summer lawn with my dog in her arms.

"Come back!" I called. "Zoe Louise! Wait up!"

But she wouldn't wait, and even worse, she stopped for an instant to put Oscar down and he trotted along after her. I didn't like him loose and free here. What if I couldn't catch him? What if he got lost here? "Don't put him down! Hold him!"

But she didn't listen to me. Even though I was frightened for Oscar I was surprised, too, surprised at how quickly he ran and romped as he hadn't done in years. He looked trim and happy. I slowed to a walk, pressing my hand into the pain that pierced my side. "I'll kill you, Zoe Louise, I swear."

She waited for me then in the middle of the field, and Oscar sat at her feet panting stupidly. She just kept grinning at me.

"So you're not dead yet," I muttered once I was near enough.

She looked at me strangely, and although I thought I saw a strange flicker of understanding pass across her eyes, she didn't seem to know what I was talking about. Here, in her clean dress and party excitement, she had no idea what was in store. It was only in my time, gazing into my eyes, that she let herself glimpse whatever it was that was about to come.

"Let's go to the bluffs and see if Papa is coming. We can see the road from there and maybe his carriage." She took my hand and tugged me along. I couldn't take my eyes off Oscar. His coat was shiny and his eyes were big and clear. I had never known him this young.

"Does Oscar look different to you?" I asked her.

She looked down at him as we walked and squinted. "I don't know. I can barely see him. He's as clear as glass."

That wasn't how I saw him. "Do I look different?" I asked, suddenly wondering.

"You look like a dead person," she answered.

I stopped short and she laughed and slipped her arm through mine.

"I'm only kidding," she said, coaxing me along. "You look just like always, like the older you, only I can see the sky behind you in your eyes, and you kind of disappear from the knees down."

I looked down at my feet and concentrated on them. I realized they were not touching the ground as I walked, so I thought thickness to them, sent strength down there, and I saw them begin to pulsate with a faint warmth. We kept moving along with Oscar leading the way.

The field behind the house led to a small wooded stretch that was cut by a rough path, and there, where I knew houses to be in my world, was a dirt road, and beyond that, unprotected by a guardrail or signs, were the island's steep bluffs exposed and open to us.

Zoe Louise broke free from me and ran ahead again. It was windy up there, the bluffs dropping sharply below us, and from the top I could see the rocks below, the stretch of woods that led to the shore of the bright bay, and through the woods, here and there, a patch of road would shine through. PopPop had told me the bluffs were leftovers from an ice age, and I had always imagined an unyielding block of ice sliding along on its own meltings—a puddle no thicker than a page of a book, he had said—that pressed into the land, shearing off trees, tearing down layers of soil, and leaving its impression carved into the land.

"Come away from there," I told Zoe Louise.

She was pacing right on the edge, along the dirt, with Oscar beside her. She pointed down to the woods.

"Oscar, here boy!" I begged.

"We'll be able to see from here when Papa is coming. Do you think the pony will be walking? Or do you think he'll bring him in a wagon? Do you think he'll be big enough for me to ride right away?"

"Zoe Louise, please come away from the edge!"

"Or will I have to wait till the pony grows?"

Now imagine this. Imagine that time is no longer the straight line that you're used to, but a curling ribbon turning back on itself over and over, spiraling downwards through all eternity, repeating, returning, curling, and you will know how I saw Zoe Louise that moment from all directions—the ground cracking, her turning to smile at me, Oscar scampering away, her turning back to point out at the road, the dust and dirt spilling down the side of the bluff, her shading her eyes, the ground dropping from beneath her so suddenly that her toes pointed in midair like a dancer's, and curling back again, her turning to smile at me, Oscar scampering, the dust, her toes, her turning to point, to smile.

And I, a ghost, bound by no rules of this particular place in time, curled back on myself, stepped backwards in my mind. "Do you think the pony will be walking?" she had asked, and here in this spiral I reached out and, concentrating on my arms and my chest, I flung myself at her, tackled her, and threw us both back onto the grass.

"Zoe!" she scolded. "What are you doing? My dress! My pretty party dress!"

We sat up and she started beating the dirt off her dress. Oscar jumped up with his front paws on her shoulders and tried to lick her face, but she threw him from her. "Get away!" she yelled. "Now Momma will be furious. Look what you've done."

"But the bluff was giving way," I told her. "It was about to break off and take you with it."

Zoe Louise wouldn't listen to me. "Oh, I hate you! I hate you! Now everything is ruined. Look at my dress! Look at it! I never want to see you again. Go on. Go home. You've ruined everything!"

Zoe Louise stood and shook off more dirt and grass and began to cry when she saw the grass stains smudged all down her side. Oscar and I just sat there on the grass and watched as she stormed away towards the house. The wind blew gently over the bluffs and the light, I noticed, was as it had been that first day I had been back there in past time. Clear and sparkling. As we sat there a hunk of the bluff where Zoe Louise had been standing broke away, and we listened to it crumble down the side into the rocks below.

I gathered Oscar onto my lap and hugged him close. "I think I did it, Oscar. I think I saved her life. Maybe she won't be dead anymore."

Oscar smelled so good there with me on the grass, I buried my face in his neck. "I like you better fat, Oscar. There's more to love." He broke from my hold and ran in funny pug circles, with his tail tucked between his legs, round and round, growling a sort of pug laughter deep in his throat. I pounded the ground around me and he ran more and more, faster and faster until I couldn't catch him. I got worried and sat stone still. He ran and ran, growling and snorting. But I wouldn't move. Finally he drew close, cautiously sniffing, creeping, and I pounced. Taking him in my arms, I stood up and we headed back. The grass was gently trampled where we had cut across the field before and I followed the same path, but this time my feet were faint visions and even carrying Oscar I didn't bend the tiniest blade of grass.

* * *

I didn't put Oscar down again until we were safe in our own kitchen, in our own time with the African violets in the window, and the table set for dinner. I felt Oscar grow fat and old as we came down the staircase, but as I set him down in the kitchen, there was a look of contentment on his face, like that of an old man who has just had one last dance with a pretty woman. I ran water in his bowl, and as I put it down my grandmother called.

"Is that you, Zoe, dear? My goodness, where have you been?"

"In the playhouse," I answered as she came into the kitchen carrying one of the old newspapers.

"All day? I called and called. Can't you hear me with the door closed?"

"Guess not. I'm sorry. I was reading those newspapers." I glanced at the clock and was startled to see how late it had gotten, how much time had passed.

"Well, I'd like you to make the salad tonight, dear, while I make the gravy and the biscuits."

"Sure, Grandma." I started taking the vegetables from the refrigerator. I felt so light and free, so hopeful, thinking maybe I had saved Zoe Louise's life that very afternoon there on Bluff Drive. Maybe I had. Maybe I had. I felt joyful.

"Grandma?"

"Yes?"

"What was Oscar like when he was young?"

She turned to look at him a moment, recollecting. "Hmm. Well, he was much thinner for one."

"Was he faster?"

"Yes, that he was. He used to run around the rooms. You must remember that. How he'd take a dish towel and make us all chase him."

I did. "Was he happier?"

"Happier, I don't know. He was young-happy then, like he's old-happy now. Old Oscar here's had a happy life. None better, right, old boy?"

She scratched his face and he leaned into her.

I turned to the cucumbers on the counter and began scraping them in long, slow peels. I could hear her settle down behind me at the table, the pages of a newspaper rustling. I sliced the cucumbers into thin coins and sprinkled them in the salad bowl. PopPop called from the other room.

"Listen to this! *Abraham Bendl, formerly of Jergen County, and new to this area, was found hanged in his small cottage out by Clarence Cove last weekend. Authorities are trying to locate his next of kin.*" PopPop came and stood in the doorway. He was holding an old newspaper gingerly in his fingers as he finished. "*Anyone knowing anything at all about Mr. Bendl is asked to contact Sheriff Wilkens. Burial was held quietly on Monday at the rear of Grace Churchyard.* You know what that is?"

We looked at him blankly. I suddenly realized that both my grandparents had been poring over the old newspapers I had left stacked on the cellar floor.

"That's that small brown tombstone in the cemetery that's set off by itself," PopPop reminded us. "Has the initials A. B., right? And a rough-cut design like the knot in a rope."

"That's right!" Grandma said, bent studiously over her own newspaper. "My goodness. Abraham Bendl. Hanged and buried. Wonder if they ever found his people. Here. Listen to this one. *Seeking gentle housekeeper to care for new baby and household, along with cook and yardman. Ten dollars a month plus board.* Ten dollars! Can you imagine such a thing. And look! The ferry was a penny! They've posted the schedule."

I looked over Grandma's shoulder at the old yellowed newsprint and the small black drawing of a ferry, with a neat list beneath it of scheduled departures and arrivals.

"These are wonderful," Grandma said, patting the paper as she set it down, "but I'll never get another blessed thing done as long as they are in this house!" She pulled the flour bin open and carefully measured out two cups of flour in a bowl while I sliced open the red tomatoes and licked their juice from my fingers.

* * *

After dinner, not one of us wanted to leave the table. There among the biscuit crumbs and dirty knives, forks and piled plates, we lingered over the spread papers, reading funny and sad events to each other, and trying to top the last story heard. It was like eating sweet chocolate chips right from the bag before they were folded into cookie batter. We couldn't stop. The sky grew dark, the food dried and cracked on our dishes. I didn't even count the bongs on the clock right before PopPop read the next one. PopPop's voice was soft and the kitchen light over him shone gently on his balding head. I turned to stone where I sat.

"Condolences and heartfelt sorrow are extended to the LaBarge family of Helen Road this week — that's this road — *at the tragic death of their young daughter, Zoe Louise."* I felt PopPop glance at me at the mention of my name, but my eyes had turned to skimming stones. *"A devastating fire was confined to the kitchen area by local firemen and volunteers who had gathered at the house for a birthday celebration. While both LaBarge children were in the kitchen when the fire began, only the younger escaped, and the elder perished in the flames."*

PopPop looked up suddenly at Grandma. "La-Barge, LaBarge," he repeated. "Isn't that the original family who lived here in this house?"

"Yes, I think so," Grandma said softly.

"Then it was this house, on Helen Road," he

said, looking around the kitchen, at the floor, the ceiling. "I've never detected any fire damage here."

We were all so still as if our movements would fan a flame to life. Suddenly I remembered the sharp smell of burnt wood that time I had seen Zoe Louise's mother in her room with her funeral dress hanging on the wall.

PopPop went on. "*The cause of the fire at this report was as yet unknown. Zoe Louise LaBarge would have celebrated her eleventh birthday on the day of her untimely death. Memorial service was held on Thursday at the Townbridge Lutheran Church.*"

"Oh, how terribly sad, Joe. In this very room."

"It was a long time ago, Frances. Don't go getting carried away now."

"Isn't it a strange coincidence though. Remember that name? Zoe Louise? Do you remember, Zoe?" Grandma had reached across the table and touched my hand. I forced myself to look at her and nod.

"That was Zoe's imaginary friend. Remember, Joe? 'Zoe Louise likes pink.' 'Zoe Louise wants cherries.' 'Zoe Louise went home.' 'Where's Zoe Louise?' Remember?"

"Vaguely," PopPop answered, folding up the old newspaper and standing. He stretched and yawned.

"Well, I'm going to pack up these newspapers for tonight," Grandma said, "before we suddenly discover ourselves still here at sunup. Zoe, you do the dishes, my dear. And don't forget to cover up the pie."

Then I was all alone in the kitchen. The refrigerator hummed softly. Oscar snored beneath the table. A soft summer breeze was coming in the window. And I got up from the table, walked across the room to the back staircase. I opened the door, stepped inside and in the darkness, I went to find her.

I didn't even turn the knob on
the upstairs landing. I just passed through the door
like walking through a curtain of strung beads. I
was as clear and as smooth as new varnish. I could
hear voices from where I stood on the upstairs
landing, many voices and laughter, the sounds of
people gathered together for a party. There were
children's voices whirling through the rooms, and
the voices of men pouring drinks, and the voices
of women passing trays and serving food. Upstairs
in the hall by me, I could hear the quiet breathing
of a man. Soundlessly, I passed along the hall to
the sound, to my grandparents' room, and I entered
where I had seen Zoe Louise's mother crying that
night. What night? Had it happened already? Was
it yet to come? I didn't smell burnt wood. There
was no black dress on the wall.

A handsome black-haired man sat on the edge of the bed, staring darkly into space. He focused on nothing, appearing to be as much of a ghost as I was. While he stared, he fiddled with his cuffs and I drew closer to him. I had never seen such a handsome man. His long ringless fingers were smooth and brown, almost like a woman's, but his nails were square and even, strong. His dark hair swirled in soft curls about his head, and his eyes were pale and deep like Zoe Louise's. There was a fine dark shadow on his cheeks. I thought of PopPop. When he needed a shave, his gray-and-brown beard stuck out all scraggly and rough from dry cheeks, but this man's beard was growing like new velvet from a fine, porcelainlike skin.

Not thinking, I reached out and touched his cheek, ran my fingers along his cheekbone, and finally cupped his jaw in my hand. As I did so, he froze, his fingers caught in midair, free of his cuff buttons. So slowly—he must have felt my touch somehow—he lifted his hand to his cheek and gently cupped it over my fingers. I didn't dare move. He couldn't see me. He was staring right through me, but I knew he was thinking about his cheek being touched. His eyes closed and I waited. I was suddenly afraid I might become visible to him, that he would see this strange child from another time at his bedside stroking his cheek.

There were footsteps, a riotous clomping up the stairs. Louder and louder. His eyes opened and he looked to the door as he straightened his stiff white collar.

"We want to see the pony now, Papa! Now! Now! Now!"

It was Oliver, straddling a broomstick pony, and although I could tell he'd been dressed nicely and carefully, one shirttail flapped behind him and he was flushed and sweaty. Mr. LaBarge stood and walked to a tall wooden closet. He acted as if Oliver were as invisible as I was.

"Now, Papa! Please, oh, now!"

"Where is your mother, Oliver? And fix your shirt."

"She's downstairs with Uncle Thomas and Aunt Phoebe." He struggled frantically with his shirt. "And Mr. Handel is setting up the croquet set, but I told him not to because Zoe Louise might want to ride the pony all around the yard—"

"Come here, Oliver."

Oliver went and stood before his father and endured while he was tucked and prodded and brushed off, and then his father ran his long fingers through the boy's hair. "Your mother said that first we will have the cake and sing "Happy Birthday," and then— once the cake is served to everyone—then we will bring out the pony for the children."

"For the children? Will we *all* get to ride him?"

"Of course."

"But it's Zoe Louise's pony."

"Your sister will be generous, I'm sure."

Oliver's little face stormed over. "What's generous?"

"Generous is your mother and I will make sure Zoe Louise gives you a turn."

Oliver brightened and began bouncing around the room, the broomstick pony dragging between his legs. "Giddap, giddap."

More rumbling on the stairs. A voice I knew. Knew so well. She bolted into the room. "Papa! Everyone's waiting for you. Everything's ready!"

At the very instant that Zoe Louise saw me, her father turned back to his closet and pulled out a pale linen jacket. He brushed it off slowly, deliberately. She was glaring at me.

"Zoe Louise, I have just returned from a long trip. I'm weary and dirty. I'd like a few minutes to wash up and put on some fresh clothes. Then I will be down."

"Giddap, giddap."

"Papa, make him stop." Zoe Louise stamped her foot and pouted.

Mr. LaBarge took both children firmly in hand and led them to the door. "I will be down when I come down. Go play."

Their whining and complaining disappeared behind the door as their father closed it. He rubbed his cheeks roughly with one hand and went back to the closet. I watched as he stared at himself for a moment in the mirror tacked to the door. Then he took down a shaving mug and a razor.

There was a pitcher and a bowl of steaming water on the oak dresser, and as he lathered up his shadowed cheeks I passed unnoticed through the door. I knew he would be a while. The people's voices I'd heard earlier were coming mostly from outdoors, from the back lawn. I stood on the landing and watched out the window. A delicate breeze cooled the warming sun, and it seemed everyone was dressed in flowing white — white skirts and bustles and white hats and bonnets, white gloves and even a couple of white parasols. There were flowers everywhere, and a table set up with a pink punch and sparkling glasses, and children ran in and out of the long skirts and randomly placed wicker chairs.

I floated down the stairs and saw two women in conversation on the brocade sofa. One clutched a lace fan in her hand. A long thin dog lay at her feet.

"Hush! Hush!" It was Zoe Louise's voice.

I could hear the whispers in the kitchen. I didn't even go around through the dining room to reach her. I passed right through the wall, the plaster, the wood and entered the kitchen to see Zoe Louise and Oliver bent over the table where the heavy pink oil lamp stood beside a huge chocolate birthday cake.

Zoe Louise's dress was rumpled and stained, but I could tell by the wet spots that someone had fussed over it and tried to get some of the stains out. She put her hand on her hip and scowled when she saw me. In her thoughts, so Oliver could not hear, I heard her say, *Go home, foolish girl, you've ruined my birthday dress. I'm not going to let you ruin my cake, too.*

"Don't stay in this room, Zoe Louise," I told her. "Come with me now."

She ignored me and turned back to the cake. Oliver was sticking the candles in the top layer.

"Eleven candles, right?" he asked.

"Come show me the pony," I begged.

"And one to grow on," she told him, pointing to each, counting to be sure.

"Zoe Louise, please. You will die in here."

"Oh, stop it," she said, seizing the remaining candles from Oliver and sticking the rest in the icing herself.

"Please. Come with me." I tried to get a grip on her arm, but she kept shaking me off, concentrating on her cake.

"Now," she was saying to Oliver, "we'll light

the candles. That way they'll have to sing Happy Birthday right now, right this minute, and Papa will *have* to come down, and Momma will be angry, but I'll blow out the candles and then the cake can be served. Then you know what comes next, Oliver!"

"Giddap, giddap," he sang, trotting around the room.

My transparent body was taking on a weird vibration. It was fear. Fear with no fingers to make tremble, fear with no eyes to make tear. Fear with no defenses, no body to absorb it and protect me. I was drenched in terror and, wasted this way in an awful foreboding, no amount of pulling or clutching at Zoe Louise could make her move. My hands and fingers only passed through every part of her.

She ignored me. The candles in place, she went to the drawer and came back to the table with a small box of wooden matches. "Now I'll light them, Oliver, and you—"

"Oh, dear God, no! Zoe Louise, please listen to me—"

"And as soon as they're lit, Oliver, you yell out the window and tell everyone to come in—"

"Can't you hear me? Can't you hear anything I say?"

She rubbed the match awkwardly across the bottom of the box, and it did not light.

117

"Should I call them now?" Oliver asked.

"Not yet, not yet."

Again she rubbed the match along the bottom, only this time a little flame leaped up, and I watched in alarm as she lit one candle after another, one, two, three —

"Oh, Zoe Louise! I beg you! Please!" I was screaming now, throwing myself against her, tearing at her dress, her braids, but nothing was working. It was like trying to move through water.

— four, five, six, seven —

"Now should I?" he asked.

"Oliver! Be patient! I'll tell you when."

— eight, nine, ten, eleven —

"All right," she said, as she lit the final candle, "now you can call them."

As Zoe Louise said that, one fat candle near the edge, the one nestled in thick chocolate icing, leaned out slowly, unnoticed, and Oliver, leaping with joy, circled once more around the table before he ran to the window. "Giddap! Giddap!" And his broom-stick pony, dancing between his legs, caught on the lace of the long linen tablecloth that draped the kitchen table. It gave a hard tug as he turned to the window, toppling the heavy pink oil lamp and also the one fat candle that was perched in the thick icing.

And now, the entire table — flaming cake, fallen

lamp, and oil-soaked tablecloth — went up in a blaze of heat and light. Oliver cried out and disappeared behind the flames, while Zoe Louise swatted at the flames, trying to slip the cake from the table. I saw little flames biting at her skirt.

I was powerless, and knew that as long as this fear enveloped me I was as weak as smoke. Nothing I did worked. I just passed through Zoe Louise like a wave of anxiety. I had to shake the fear, had to strip myself of the terror that possessed me, and taking an instant, knowing an instant here could be a year somewhere else, I slowly took the time I needed — to think of something else, anything else, something empty of fear.

For some reason I thought of my mother. There was no fear there. Anger, maybe confusion, but never fear. I saw her standing out back by the raspberries with me that day. It was her instead of Zoe Louise's mother. It was my own mother so close to me, her raspberry bucket passing through my arm, her cheek so close to mine, and standing in the burning kitchen, the flames licking around me, I reached out to my mother and placed my arms around her and held her. I felt her arms go around me too, felt her nuzzle her face in the crook of my neck. We were solid to each other, present, real. I was sobbing. I wanted never to stop, never to let go, yet as we held on so tightly to each other, I felt my feet moving, felt my feet making their way across the burning kitchen. Zoe Louise was in my arms and it was Zoe Louise who was crying and choking. I held her as tight as I could. My arms were thick and real. I could hear men shouting, women screaming.

My hand was solid on the doorknob to the back staircase. It turned easily for me, and the door opened to us. Holding Zoe Louise tightly against me, I pulled her inside and quickly closed the door against the heat, the flames, and the horrible smoke.

Zoe Louise was gasping for air, choking, and sobbing. Her singed hair scraped my face. Smoke bled under the door, engulfing us in its ghostly touch. "Momma! Momma!" she gasped, and when Zoe Louise pulled the door open a gust of heat and smoke pushed her back. She slammed it shut and stood there swaying.

"Come with me, come with me," I whispered. "I'll keep you safe."

But for the first time I don't think Zoe Louise could hear me or see me anymore. It was clear she thought she was all alone, all alone in the staircase of her burning home.

"Zoe Louise! Try to hear me. Try to hear what I say."

But she stared at the bottom door, trembling and rubbing her burnt hands on her sooty skirt.

"You must come with me," I coaxed. I slipped my arm around her waist and tried to pull her up the steps. But she acted like an invisible snake had tried to encircle her. She beat me off, her whimperings turning to breathless screams.

"It's me, it's only me." I could feel her terror in the staircase. It was like the smoke seeping under the door, the heat that was pushing in from the kitchen wall. She beat against me with her fists and her feet. Her breathing was uneven and difficult, and then I watched her go limp and topple to the ground.

I was not all that much bigger than Zoe Louise, and I struggled to lift her off the floor and out of the smoke. I couldn't pick her up no matter how I tried. If only she would help, if only she would hold on. Finally I knew all I could do was drag her up the staircase a step at a time. From the other side of the door I could hear men shouting while a roaring fire licked the walls. Grasping Zoe Louise under each arm, I got above her on the steps and pulled.

Sometimes a terrible indescribable dread comes in a dream. A terrible sense of *oh, no, not again, not this*. And now, as in that dream, I felt it again, and every spark in my soul cried out—*please no, not now, not this*, because a heaviness was pushing me down, a soundless current that had held me back once before in this very staircase. But now instead of Zoe Louise clinging to me, trying to call me back, she was lifeless under my hands, and while heat and fire grabbed at her from the bottom, time crushed us from the top.

With all my strength I wrapped my arms around her and pulled her up just one more step, just one more step, one step away from the heat, until we were in the middle of the stairwell. My hands felt like lead weights at the ends of my arms, but as gently as I could, I cupped them over her mouth and nose. A storm wind of time pressed me down and when I could no longer hold my head up, I laid my face heavily against her head. She was barely breathing and on the other side of the wall I could hear screams, her mother calling her name over and over. But I held on to Zoe Louise, balanced her there between death and time with all the strength I had . . . and, I know now, with all the love I had.

12

Without clocks or tides to measure it, time seems not to exist, except for its heavy hand pressing down, so I don't know how long Zoe Louise and I stayed in the stairwell that afternoon. We didn't move, neither up nor down, until suddenly the stairwell was filled with light. The door opened at the bottom and a man was there looking up.

"She's here! Here she is!" he shouted, and he ran up to us, lifted Zoe Louise easily from my arms, and carried her down the stairs. Others joined him, touching her dangling foot, brushing the hair from her face. I followed like the ghost I was. Through the kitchen, down the dark-green steps to the lawn, where he laid her down and knelt over her.

Her mother came running, running, running, and

being a ghost I saw from all sides, I saw her coming towards us, her arms outstretched, I saw her running away from me to a daughter who lay unconscious on the grass, and I also saw inside her own eyes, running, running, towards death or life, death or life, she thought as she ran. "Zoe!" Her screams filled the oak trees. "Zoe! Zoe Louise!"

She threw herself on the grass near the man whose ear was pressed to Zoe Louise's chest. "She's alive," he said. "Yes, yes."

"Oh, dear God, oh, dear God." I watched as she gathered her child up in her arms and rocked her. And I watched as Zoe Louise lifted her arm and looped it around her mother's neck. I watched as her father came running, his fancy clothes stained black with water and smoke. And I watched as Oliver stood off alone in the distance, his eyes big with uncertainty.

Like the shadow of a harmless afternoon cloud skimming over the earth, I left the cluster of people behind and passed over the summer grasses to Oliver. I circled him. I thought of PopPop nudging Oscar out the door with his foot. Gently, firmly, I leaned into Oliver that way. I leaned into him and I pressed, and pressed. Reluctantly his feet gave in. I leaned into him, cupping my soul around him, till he was running to his sister, over the lawns, beneath the trees, and when he reached her, his father lifted him into the air and held him close.

I watched as Zoe Louise sat up, and the voices and sounds became dim to me. I circled around her and settled at her feet. There were no sounds. People moved and talked and laughed in relief, but I saw only their lips moving.

Total silence.

I searched out Zoe Louise's eyes. "Zoe Louise?" I whispered, but she didn't respond. Didn't see me there. "Zoe Louise?"

I knew then for sure it was over.

And Zoe Louise was alive.

The staircase never worked again. I open the door at night sometimes and stare up the stone steps, looking for daylight beneath the top door. Once I even walked up the steps and came out same day, same house, same century in my own upstairs. Whatever it was that had let me travel back to Zoe Louise was gone forever. And yet I remembered her saying how once she came looking for me and I was grown and I no longer saw her. So sometimes I sit perfectly still in my room or in the playhouse and try to feel her nearby. But for me it is over.

Except for one thing, one strange thing that I'll never be able to explain. The season's first light snow was falling the morning my mother appeared for her next brief, unexpected visit. The playhouse had been repaired and closed up for the winter, and the old newspapers that had long ago lost their interest were once again back in the cellar storage closet where they'd been forgotten.

Lunch was over, the dishes were dried, and this time she said she thought she'd like to walk in the woods, in the snow, to search for seed pods and pine cones. She didn't ask me to go with her, but when she eased her black cape over her head, and slipped her hands into her patched woolen gloves, I, too, put my coat on, and without a word followed her out the back door, down the steps, and out to the snake woods, or what I knew now to be the remains of a beautiful garden from the past.

My mother led the way, her cape's huge, soft hood draped around her head and face, and her feet pressing footprints smaller than mine into the snow. She stopped here and there and with a stick turned over clumps of sticks and snow, leaves and ice.

I wandered away from her, back to see the rose-bushes.

But I couldn't find them.

"Mom," I called. "Where were they? Where were those rosebushes? I can't find them." I was deeper in the woods, past the stump, past even where I thought they might have been.

"I can't find where those memory roses were planted," I told her. "Do you remember exactly?"

"What memory roses?" she asked, coming towards me, her face as blank as a snow-laden roof.

"The rosebushes," I said impatiently. "You know. From when that little girl died."

"What little girl?"

She stood there carved in black against the white snow, all blankness.

"The little girl, remember? You told me? Zoe something. From the tombstone. The girl who died, and her mother planted the pink roses —"

Nothing. Nothing. I could see her face and she didn't know what I was talking about.

"—so they would bloom on her birthday!" I was shouting at my mother. She was staring at me.

"Zoe, what is the matter with you?"

"Don't you remember the rosebushes? They were right here!" Suddenly with relief I felt thorns tug at my jeans. "Here!" I cried. "Here they are!" I pulled at the branches and they pricked me and tore at my clothes. I was standing right in the middle of them.

"Zoe, those aren't roses. Those are raspberries. They've been there forever. Since I was a girl."

"No! They're roses. I know, I know."

My mother was beside me. She placed one hand on my shoulder and with the other helped me pull the raspberry branches off my coat. I tried to see her eyes, but the hood hid her face.

When she stood I looked into her eyes, tried to read the small print there in the back of her head. She really didn't know.

"Mommy. You don't remember?" I whispered.

"Remember what?" she asked.

And then I knew. The roses had never been here. I knew for certain now that within the borders of the present day, there had been no death. No little girl had died over a hundred years ago. And no grieved mother had planted a stand of rosebushes in her memory. But surely it was true that a little girl had once come calling for me to come see her birthday pony. I stood in my moment in time, felt my face give way, and I started to cry.

"Oh, Zoe," my mother said softly. "What's wrong?" And without my having to tell her, and maybe because she was a little crazy, she never asked again. She just wrapped her cape around me and we stood there like that, holding on to each other, like two statues maybe, yes, like two tiny statues in an antique globe, and the light snow swirled about us like forgiveness.

The memory of her leaving again that time is as clear as the breath in my hands, were I to cup my hands to my face now, it is that real, that close. I stood on the front porch late in the day, the steps covered with a light dusting of snow, and my mother hesitated by the door of her old dented car. A winter bird sounded in the bare woods like a flute down a hollow tube.

"Want to stop at the old churchyard with me before I go?" she asked.

I thought of the tombstones, the old trees, and shook my head. "Nah, that's okay."

She squinted up at me. The small setting sun was off to my left, surrounding my mother in pink airiness. "You'll be all right now, Zoe?" She waited for my answer.

I patted my bare hand on the cold wooden railing, solid railing, solid hand. I felt whole. I felt somehow like I'd come full circle. My mother had promised to come in the spring and plant a rosebush with me. And somewhere, or rather sometime long ago, I knew that a little girl who had been my friend had grown to be a woman and gone on to do things I could only imagine. I heard the clock strike five in the house.

"Zoe?"

She was just standing there.

"I'm sorry, Zo."

"For what?"

She shrugged and looked around the front yard as if she would find the answer there. "I don't know. For everything, I guess. Everything."

I smiled at her, maybe the first time I'd ever

really smiled at her in my whole life, and I backed up the stairs to the house. "It's all right," I told her and in that instant I meant it. It really was all right.

Then from the porch I watched as she got into her car and backed it around, her tires leaving fresh tracks in the snow. There were twisted blooming honeysuckle wreaths and huge pine cones piled in her back window, so thick I couldn't see her head, but I waved. I waved until I couldn't see her car anymore, and then when she was out of sight, I bolted from the porch, ran around the house, across the snow-laden lawn, through the backyard, and the white trees, over a fence, through two more yards untouched by footprints, until I reached Bluff Drive, and with the bay sparkling below like ancient days, I stood there alone—alone and whole—and I waved wildly when I saw her car pass through the trees.